Comments on Jerry Craven's Writing

Novelist Ernest Gaines' assessment in choosing *Women of Thunder* as first place winner in a national contest:

It is a story of love and adventure, of reality and fantasy. The characters, the places they visit and the action are real. The language is simple and true. It is written so well that it holds our interest and keeps us turning the pages.

This writer has great talent.

"Craven manages to blend almost mystical awe with whimsical bemusement, especially when he deposits the most unlikely figures in the heart of strange surroundings." —David Bowles reviewing *The Wild Part*

"Jerry Craven populates his stories with a variety of believable and appealing characters, measuring the mix of humor and seriousness in balanced proportions." —*World Literature Today* commenting on *Tiger, Tiger and Other Stories*

"A lifetime of associating with fascinating characters and experiencing the world in exotic locales such as Venezuela and Malaysia (not to mention Texas), has provided rich fodder for Jerry Craven's twenty-plus books of fiction, poetry, and nonfiction." —David A. Faught reviewing *Saving a Songbird*

The Wild Part "brought to mind Joseph Conrad's *Heart of Darkness* and its questions about civilized society and racism." —Carol Smallwood's review of *The Wild Part*

"This tale is full of mystery and danger and exotica. It is a book you won't be able to stop reading once you've started." —Jane Robert Woods commenting on *Searching for Rama's Spear*

"Jerry Craven's *Women of Thunder* reminds us of Gabriel García-Márquez's fiction." —Roberto Bonazzi reviewing *Women of Thunder*

Jerry Craven, a writer of literary fiction with a flare the dramatic, offers his best writing in this book.

In *Ceremonial Stones of Fire* you will meet

Steven Duck, a Malaysian street dealer in coins determined to teach an American the way commerce can numb the spirit

Joko, a man in Bali who understands the true nature and danger of magic pigs and humans

Weng, who must contemplate the moral implications of revenge upon a pirate

and other sympathetic characters who deal with what life brings them in what to us are exotic lands and events.

Craven based these stories on real experiences and people he knew in Malaysia, Singapore, Bali, Nepal, Thailand, and along the pirate coasts of the Straits of Malacca.

Ceremonial Stones of Fire

Ceremonial Stones of Fire

Jerry Craven

ANGELINA
RIVER
PRESS

ISBN: 978-0-9987364-0-2

Library of Congress Control Number: 2017934583

Angelina River Press, LLC

Fort Worth, Texas

Acknowledgments

For their help in teaching me their language, I am grateful to many students of Institut Teknologi MARA. I taught them basics of writing English; they helped me learn the basics of speaking bahasa Malaysia. I thank Lionel K.H. Low, who speaks several languages fluently, including English, for tutoring me in both tennis and the cultural mores of Malaysians.

Thanks to the editors of these journals for publishing some of the stories in this book: *Carve Magazine, CCTE Studies, Concho River Review, Haunts Magazine, REAL: RE Arts & Letters, riverSedge,* and *Thema.*

Other Books from Angelina River Press

CONTENTS

New Opal Ring

Thieves caught Ed in the shadowy alley between the Hindu temple and the fishmonger's shop. They had been squatting between two cars and came popping out when he approached, three of them. "You will please to give us the wallet," one of them said.

"And the camera," another added, "so we will not break arm." Ed turned to run, but a fourth thief blocked his way. When he turned to face the three, they were upon him. One jerked the camera from his hand, another removed his wallet from his hip pocket. The third was clawing at his watch when a shadowy figure sprang upon the thieves.

The first blow from the shadow drew a grunt from the man jerking at Ed's watch. The second blow hit the face of another thief. Ed stood, astonished by the chaos, the swinging fists, growls and thumping sounds. By the time he decided to try throwing a few punches, it was too late. A man behind him shoved Ed to the ground, and the thieves ran.

Ed found himself lying beside his rescuer. "Are you all right?" Ed asked.

"Better than I deserve after such a foolish act." The man sat up. "We made them run like pilchards before a net, no?"

"No. You made them run." Ed helped the man to his feet. "All I did was stand there like a fool and get robbed. You're a brave man, and I thank you." The two walked toward the lighted street in front of the temple. "Your nose is bleeding. Here." Ed gave him a handkerchief. The man applied it to his nose.

"Thanks. I amb Steben Duck."

"I'm Ed, and I'm really glad to meet you, Steven." In the light, Ed examined the man. He was of Chinese descent, of medium height, and about 28 or 30 years old, Ed guessed. Steven's clothes said he was accustomed to affluence, though he was dusty and had blood splattered on the front of his shirt. He wore a watch and a gold ring set with an opal—items that looked to be of more worth than Ed's camera and wallet.

"I have always been afraid of violence." Steven dabbed at the blood on his nose. "When I hit those men in the alley, I was pretending they were the bullies of my youth. Pang Wah. Lee Chang. Big boys who once terrified me." He grinned.

"Good god, fellow. They knocked out some of your upper teeth."

"No." Steven laughed. "Those few upper teeth I lost to a Mercedes truck on the Federal Highway."

"Suppose we find a place to see to that nose?" Ed looked up and down the street.

"That way. On Petaling Street. We can go to the Sun Wah coffee house. A little ice and something to drink, and all will be straight again."

Ed followed Steven. Twice Steven stumbled and Ed caught his arm. Ed noticed his new friend had a stiff leg.

They walked past old men playing some sort of board game, past several street people lying on the sidewalk, past the Mandarin Hotel. As they approached Petaling Street, the sidewalk became more crowded with Chinese. Food stalls lined one side of the street, and merchants of various types did business on the covered walkway across the street. Ed saw cobblers repairing shoes in the gutter, fortune tellers looking at elaborate charts with customers squatting around them, men selling caged birds, and several fierce-looking fellows sitting in lotus positions, displays of jewelry and colored stones and coins and icons of Buddha on small carpets before them.

When they reached Petaling Street, Steven turned to announce, "This is known as Chinatown. Here you will find capitalism in its most rabid form."

The street was closed to automobiles—and almost to people, Ed thought. Vendors stood behind make-shift tables, small stalls, and upon scraps of carpet covered with merchandise. Shirts and dresses hung from lines stretched between poles so that Ed had to duck beneath them. Several stalls sold watches. One entrepreneur had surrounded a parking meter with a display of brassieres. As Ed and Steven wound their way through the maze of merchandise, people tried to get them to look at their ware. "Rolex watch, boss? Calvin Kline pants, genuine, you want? Old coins—special price for you. This from Tibet—genuine prayer wheel."

Ed thought the merchandising on Petaling Street wasn't all that foreign to his own businesses. Sure, he had attractive stores in Dallas to sell his goods, but the differences were superficial. The staff of his women's ready-wear stores didn't go out into the street to hawk clothing, but they used a number of subtle techniques to get people to buy. Ed decided the main difference between the brand of capitalism practiced by his Fashion Corners stores and the hawkers on Petaling Street was in style. Their goals were the same: to exchange goods for money.

His trip to Kuala Lumpur was based on a desire to sell more dresses and other clothing items to women in Dallas. The Malaysian factory his corporation owned that produced batik skirts, dresses, and blouses had fallen in production in the last several months. And the factory's manager had been turning in some rather odd items on his list of miscellaneous expenses.

Like the goats, for example. Ed grimaced at the memory.

The Sun Wah coffee house looked to Ed like a garage converted into a café. When Steven entered, several people got up, giving their table to Steven and Ed. "They think you are a customer come to do business with me," Steven explained. He said some words in Cantonese to the proprietor, who vanished and returned with a cloth and some ice. "Out there," Steven gestured to the street, "you see the traps people set for themselves." He applied the cloth and ice to his nose. "Your handkerchief is in sad shape. Perhaps ruined. Did the robbers take anything from you?"

"My wallet. And a camera. I lost some of the cash I brought with me, and my credit cards. Fortunately I have the habit of keeping most of my cash in this," he took out a small leather case, "with my business cards."

"Not a bad deal, don't you think? You had a little adventure, and all it cost you was a leather pouch stuffed with plastic and colored papers printed with the pictures of men who are dead. And the camera. But cameras are everywhere, and quite cheap."

Ed stared at Steven in astonishment. An adventure? Getting mugged? Losing—he did some quick calculations and winced at the amount—more money than he cared to name. And that was an adventure? But why not? Steven thought the incident interesting, and he got his nose bashed.

"I need to report the mugging to the police, now that we have taken care of your nosebleed."

"If you wish. But nothing will come of it."

"Is that certain?"

"Nothing is ever certain."

Ed looked at Steven, trying to determine what he meant. The tone of his voice said he wasn't talking only about the robbery. "How did you get a name like Steven Duck?"

"My real name is Tung Chung Low. Or maybe Low Tung Chung, if you use the Chinese arrangement rather than the American. But I prefer to be called Steven Duck."

"May I ask why without being insulting or too familiar?"

"You may ask. It is because Tung is such a common name. Or maybe because there was an obscure English peasant named Steven Duck who once commanded the attention of the queen for his poetry. Also because a tongue is a hideous thing inside the mouths of snakes and water buffalo."

"You like to joke."

"Not at all. I like to experiment. You Americans are so serious— but then so was I, once. When I managed a computer business in

14

Jahore Baru. That was another life, though. Did you ever read the poetry of Steven Duck?"

"I never heard of him."

"Few have. Do you know the difference between kinky and perverse?"

"Is this a joke?"

"Kinky is a single feather. Perverse is the whole duck. I am the whole duck, now. Perverse. Not in a sexual way, though, for the name is just a metaphor.

"So you're perverse. In what way?"

"Chinese work too much. I once did. But so what if I became wealthy? Not by your standards, perhaps, but wealthy. I hated computers, hated what I did each day. Now I work as I wish. I sell coins. The job pays, but not in wealth. I travel—to Bangkok, to Singapore—even once to Mandalay, in Burma. I spent two weeks collecting coins from the silver smiths on the Indonesian island of Bali, around Ubud. They take wonderful Dutch guilder from the last two centuries and ruin them by soldering them into necklaces and belts. I also spent much time going through old temples and swimming at Kuta Beach. One could do worse than collect coins in southeast Asia."

"So you gave up a lucrative job, a secure job as a business manager to deal in coins?" The idea seemed absurd to Ed.

"Lucrative, yes. But lucre is sometimes filthy. Tell me about you, Ed."

"Here," Ed produced a business card, wrote "Shangri-La Hotel, room 640," on the back and handed it to Steven.

"Edward Lincoln Pitt," Steven read. "Is that the name you were born with, or do you remake yourself?"

"My original name. After my great grandfather. The family story is that the old man's name was Pittman, but when he moved from Ohio to New Mexico and set himself up as a consulting geologist, he shortened the name to Pitt. The story is that he was once a preacher."

With no more prompting, Ed began telling about his own past: a tale of years of work. He had been more or less independent since he was 14. He had always been in sales, starting out as a paper boy, going on to being a Fuller Brush salesman, a shoe salesman, manager of a shoe department in a women's clothing store, and then manager of a corporation. Ed did not mention that the corporation belonged to him, but he did talk about the long hours of work it took to make the company productive.

Then he told Steven the reason he came to Kuala Lumpur. "What?" Steven asked. "You say you came here because of declining production and because of some odd things on the local expense account? How much of a decline?"

"Six percent for three months. Approximately."

"And how much did the odd items run over budget?"

"Faisal, the manager, has always come in under budget."

"And you spent thousands of dollars on a trip here for that? Ed, you are not being honest with yourself."

"But I am." Ed tried to sound convincing. But even as he talked, he wondered if he were just rationalizing in order to be able to escape the Fashion Corners for a while. "I had this fine young manager in a shop in Plano. Brilliant. Capable. When he offered to computerize his shop, I agreed. He seemed certain to be the person I could put second in command of the entire corporation in just a few years. But he became a computer nut. He wrote programs that worked just fine, then he wrote other programs, because he fell in love with the machine in his office. He stopped caring so much about how the store did, and he let down on ordering new merchandise. I went in one day and found him playing a computer game he had written. When he became aware I was watching, he hit a special key, and a spread sheet appeared on the screen, replacing the aliens he had been zapping with tiny space ships. I had to fire the best manager I had in the stateside offices, and I never did figure out what went wrong. His interests drifted away from selling, and he became a useless employee. I'm afraid that Faisal might well be going through something similar. Not with a computer, though.

Perhaps with something in the Malay culture I know nothing about. So I have come unannounced to see if I can find the problem."

"Perhaps you came to vacation? To get away from the grind of selling, selling, selling? Malaysia is a beautiful land for vacations."

Ed considered the possibility, then said he rejected it. But he did admit that he would like to think he had come for a vacation. He had always wanted to see people living a different life from what he knew in Texas. And he had once dreamed of learning to snorkel. A foolish dream, he confessed, one carried out through buying books and magazines about snorkeling. "Most of all, I wanted to see a real, live clown fish," he said, flushing. "One of those orange spotted jobs that like to rub against the tentacles of a blubbery—"

"I have seen them in the waters of Tioman Island, off the east coast of Malaysia. The movie *South Pacific* was filmed there. It is the most beautiful place in the earth. Would you like to go there?"

"I would. But I cannot. There's too much work I must do while in Malaysia."

"You have trapped yourself just like those outside." Steven waved his hand at the riot of vendors covering the street. "The trap is an illusion."

Ed looked around the room. Men sat on cheap plastic and steel chairs beside Formica-topped tables, drinking coffee and smoking. Most had leather bags on the table in front of them or in their laps, and most were Chinese. One table in the back was surrounded by small dark men with round faces. "Who are all these people?" Ed wanted to shift the conversation to something more comfortable.

"Jobbers. Dealers in jewelry, or in old watches, or in gemstones. I am the only one who deals exclusively in old coins, though the others pick up some from time to time. We meet here to exchange news and to trade with one another. These men are less trapped than most, but they, too, are caught."

"Who are those fellows?" Ed indicated the dark men in the back.

"Burmese. They smuggle gemstones out of Burma and sell them

to jewelry makers in Kuala Lumpur and Singapore. They are trapped worse than most. They live rather miserable lives because they believe themselves to be miserable. And they believe that they are trapped. Which, of course, makes it true. Perhaps I could solve your mystery about declining production."

"Would you be interested in doing that? I would hire you as a consultant."

"I might. But on my terms. You must agree to accompany me to the home of my father and brother. It isn't far. And you must agree not to get in a hurry."

"And your fee?"

"I don't want to discuss money. If I am of help, then you can pay me, if you insist. But be aware that you owe me nothing. The Chinese have a saying: 'friends are friends, but money is money.' I would prefer to help you as a friend and for money to be that which the vendors on Petaling Street give their souls to possess."

"What could I possibly lose on a deal like that?" Ed laughed.

"If you are lucky, I will teach you to lose some of your illusions." Steven smiled and dabbed at his nose. "Wisdom comes hard. My tongue knows many wisdoms, yet my body continues to plunge into folly."

Ed was baffled, but he tried not to show it. "When will you start to work on the problem with my factory?"

"Tomorrow, perhaps. You must meet me here, at the Sun Wah, at nine in the morning for the trip to meet my brother. We will go to Crab Island."

That night Ed had a taxi take him to the police station where he filed a report on the robbery. Then he went to his room at the Shangri-La Hotel and called his home office, requesting some money be wired to him at the hotel, and he had his secretary deal with the matter of the stolen credit cards. The next morning, he returned to Petaling Street.

Near the Sun Wah, just as Steven joined him, Ed glanced at a small barrel beside the entrance to an alley. He would have let it go unnoticed but for the fact that some small something flew out of the barrel into the street. An orange peel, he decided. Then some other objects flew from the barrel: more orange peels and the spiny red husks of the rambutan fruit. "Is a monkey doing that?" he asked. "What's in there, anyway?"

"Death," Steven said. "That is a killing tong."

Ed stepped over to the barrel, much to the amusement of a man standing near it. Inside, Ed saw the headless body of a chicken thrashing about, its wings flipping out small bits of refuse.

"Wet Market." Steven indicated the alley by the barrel. Ed stepped back, feeling dizzy. He looked down the alley at stalls of meat and vegetable vendors. Several men carved up the body of a pig; others cleaned fish; still others washed vegetables. The street ran wet from blood and water.

"Want chicken?" the man by the barrel asked. "You pick, I kill. Pluck. Ver fresh, ver cheap." He pointed to a cage of live chickens.

"Let's get out of here." Ed felt the need to get as far as he could from the killing tong.

They walked to the K.L. Klang Bus station, Ed slowing his pace out of deference to Steven's limping walk. They boarded a red-and-white bus. "Ordinarily," Steven said, "I take this trip on my motorcycle. But for this once—for the sake of your heart, I thought I would take the bus instead of asking you to ride on my cycle."

On the Federal Highway, Ed was startled by the way cars, trucks, and busses passed one another with only inches to spare. Then, when the motorcycle lane joined the highway, just outside of Kuala Lumpur, he was astounded by the driving habits of the cyclists. "That guy," Ed told Steven, "reached out and drew a line in the dust on the side of this bus as he went around us."

"Yes. The cyclists drive in unexpected ways."

"And look at that. Those fellows are going between the bus and that truck, passing us both—with mere inches on each side. Those two are crazy."

"We say here that the cyclists think the white stripe between the two lanes is the motorcycle lane." Steven regarded Ed with amusement.

"Don't they know they can die?"

"They are cursed with the immortality of youth. Most of them. I like to think some are aware of how close to the edge of death they live, but perhaps that is fantasy. Look, Ed, at that family." He pointed to a cycle on which a man and a woman rode. Between them, the woman held an infant she was feeding with a bottle. "I have seen as many as five on a single motorcycle—the father with two small children in front of him and another child behind, between him and the mother."

Ed stared in amazement at the family on the cycle. The father wove in and out of the traffic like a snake; the mother gave all her attention to holding and feeding her child. "She isn't even holding on," he said.

"No. They grow up on cycles, so they have no fear of riding them."

"But don't they die? Aren't there many accidents?"

"Daily. But why should that be a deterrent? Isn't death always something that happens to someone else?"

"And you ride your cycle on this highway?"

"Now, yes."

The bus wound its way through Shah Alam, past a gigantic blue mosque, past a small lake landscaped with walks, foot bridges, trees, and flowering shrubs; through neighborhoods of lavish homes with red-tiled roofs; past a chocolate factory, a brewery, and other industrial buildings, picking up and letting off workers; then returned to the Federal Highway, going by a mosque with golden minarets. The grassy esplanade in the center of the highway blossomed with an abundance of flowers, and men who looked to Ed like terrorists with their heads and faces wrapped in coarse cloth mowed the grass around the shrubs with what appeared to be portable lawn edgers. Some stood on the pavement, swinging their blades over the grass, oblivious of the vehicles zipping by, just inches from their elbows.

"Death is a close neighbor to many Malaysians," Steven said.

"They seem unaware of how close to the edge they live. But the highway is beautiful. What are those flowers, the big ones?"

"Bunga raya. The king of flowers. You would call them hibiscus, I believe. Most like bunga raya for its beauty. I like it for its wisdom. It rolls its sweetness into a rod against the darkness and spreads its color into the sun. If we would be wise, we would leave this bus and study the king of flowers."

Ed shot Steven a quick, startled glance. "You say that, and yet you would drive the Federal Highway on a motorcycle?"

"I am flawed with illusions and blessed with mortality."

Ed could make no sense at all of Steven's statement.

When the bus reached the end of the highway at Port Klang, Steven and Ed walked a short way to a pier where they stepped into a sampan. The man in the boat stood while pushing the oars, taking them to a flat-decked ferry with a canopy over it and seats that looked to Ed like church pews. When the ferry departed, a dozen other people where on board, some on the pews, some in the stern, sitting beside gunny sacks of onions and garlic. Several were young school girls wearing white dresses with blue pinafores. One girl studied a book written in Chinese characters. Ed noticed that she had an extra thumb on each hand, small useless-looking appendages below more normal-looking thumbs.

The trip to Crab Island took an hour, with the ferry going in channels between islands of mangrove swamp. The scenery for most of the trip looked to Ed like scenes from old movies he had seen of rivers in Africa.

Crab Island, Steven explained, was an island only at low tide. When the tide was in, the land vanished. The island was populated with Chinese-Malaysian fishermen who lived in houses built on stilts connected with an elaborate system of boardwalks.

When they reached the so-called island, there was no land visible. An occasional mangrove tree grew among the houses, protruding from muddy water. Those on the ferry climbed a ladder to a pier that took them to the boardwalks of the village. Ed was startled to discover the walks to be quite narrow—less than four feet—and to have no hand rails.

"That," Steven pointed to a white frame building with a number of walks leading to it, "is the only Christian church on the island. But there are a number of Buddhist temples. And there," he pointed again, "is what passes for the business district."

In the business area, the walks widened into a kind of street with a few shops on either side: grocery stores, shops for dry goods, and several open-air restaurants. The first restaurant they came to belonged to Steven's father, though his older brother, Hung, ran the business.

After feeding them a meal of boiled crab, chili prawns and rice, Hung—the only member of Steven's family on Crab Island who spoke any English, suggested he take Ed to see the biggest temple on the island. "You," he pointed at Steven, "please stay with father. Talk."

"You might not know it, Ed," Steven said, "but you came to Crab Island so you could go on a walk with Hung."

Ed found the walk to the temple harrowing. Bicycles kept going by them at absurd speeds. Ed would hear the cyclist ring a bell in warning, which meant Ed and Hung had to hurry to the edge of the walk, and the bicycle would go by them far too close and too fast to suit Ed. He felt in constant danger of falling into the murky water. Children along the way—some just barely able to walk—got similar treatment from the cyclists, though they seemed as unbothered as was Hung by what Ed regarded as coming close to falling off the edge.

"Do any of the children ever fall into the water?" He asked.

"Sometimes. Not many times," Hung said. "There the Temple."

Ed found it an impressive structure, considering the architecture on the island. It was painted in brilliant red and white, and carved dragons and birds stood on the corners of the roof. In front sat some sort of altar where the faithful left joss sticks burning, and Ed could see another, more elaborate altar inside. "We sit here," Hung said, indicating a bench beside the burning joss sticks, "and talk about Tung."

"Tung?"

"Tung Chung Low. Brother."

"Steven," Ed said.

"Yes. Brother. But him not Steven Duck. Him Tung. Him say in Cantonese to Father you hire him. That good. Since Tung bang head on highway, lose teeth, him change. Sell shop in Jahore, lose much money, become bum playing with old coins on Petaling Street. Not work no more like Chinese. Play like Malay. Change name to stupid Duck, ride motorcycle like crazy man. You hire him? That good. You help him learn work again, to be Chinese again."

"But I'm not Chinese," Ed objected.

"Not matter. Tung tell Father you work like Chinese. Maybe you nearly smart as Chinese. Tung change when truck hit car, bang head, make Tung crazy so him turn to no good bum, lazy like Malay. Him go to Kuantuan, swim with snakes, go to jungle—because why? Because it fun to smash jungle like Malay boy playing. Spend money on no good ring and watch, throw away money like water, not care. You help him?"

"I'll try. But you keep calling him Malay like that was a bad word. Aren't all of you Malaysians?"

"Malaysians, yes. But not Malay. Malay not smart, like Chinese. Chinese much superior, much smarter, and develop brain early. From using chopsticks. From reading Chinese characters, brain get very better. From learning abacus. Malay not born so smart, not develop brain. Eat with hands. Not learn abacus. No can read Chinese characters. Brain move slow, get lazy, not make money. Tung get dumb like Malay, quit work, not care for making money. You help him."

On the ferry trip back to Port Klang, Steven said, "What did you learn from talking with my brother, Hung?"

"That he is very concerned about you."

"Do you believe that? Might he be concerned with what he wants me to be and not with what I am?" Ed didn't answer, nor did Steven seem to expect him to. "Did you like him?"

"He was interesting," Ed hedged.

23

"You are diplomatic. Would you, if you could, have me be like Hung? I can see that you would not. But why not?"

Ed realized that Steven was trying to teach him something—or rather to get him to teach himself something. But what? "In some ways, I did not like Hung."

"Good. What ways? Please be aware that I will not condemn you. We do not choose our relatives, as we choose our friends."

"I guess it was all the talk about Chinese superiority and about Malays."

Steven looked disappointed, and Ed felt as if he had given the wrong answer somehow. "Hung is, unfortunately, something of a racist," Steven said. That's putting it mildly, Ed thought. "No doubt he told you I am becoming a Malay, perhaps an Indian?"

"He didn't mention Indians."

"Then he is more angry with me than I thought, for his finest contempt is saved for the Malay. In Malaysia, we have three races, and each struggles with the others. My brother thinks he is better than the Malays because he is Chinese, because he is lucky enough and clever enough to own pieces of dirt and water. Many Malays see themselves as the native sons of the land and resent other races as intruders—especially they resent the Chinese who own so much of the country. The Indian envies the political control of the Malays and the wealth of the Chinese. All are trapped in false wisdom and cursed to violence. And for what? They too often forgo love and joy in a quest for the illusion of ownership."

"You aren't a communist, are you?"

"Not at all. Communists have the same illusions but would assign ownership differently."

"Then what are you trying to teach me?"

"You must forgive me, Ed, for I lack the humility wisdom requires to serve as guru. And I get caught in paradox. Even as I study ways to lose desire, I burn with passion for freedom from yearning."

"Your brother made some accusations that I did not

24

understand." Ed hoped to move the conversation to something less obtuse. "He said you swim at Kuantuan with the snakes?"

"Yes, that is true." Steven laughed. "Kuantuan is on the east coast, on the South China Sea, which is famous for its sea snakes—small but gentle green sea creatures whose bite is more deadly than the cobra. I happen to love swimming off the beaches around Kuantuan. Hung thinks I will disturb a sea snake and be bitten to death."

"Might that happen?"

"It is possible, but unlikely. What else did he say?"

"That you play in the jungle like a Malay boy."

"Not so. I play in the jungle as did Englishmen, as some Europeans still do. They called it 'jungle bashing.' A barbaric thing, really. All you need is a large knife and a bit of pristine jungle, and you can go jungle bashing—cutting your way through it, just for the challenge of getting through. It isn't all that dangerous, though. I have seen only four cobras in the dozen or so times I have done it. What else did Hung say of me?"

"That you play instead of working, that—but I just remembered he said you once owned that computer company you said you worked for. Is that so?"

"Yes. But then, you likely own the company you work for, but you neglected to mention that fact. What else?"

"Something about buying a worthless ring, as I recall. Which is absurd—that gold ring you wear is set with one of the finest Australian opals I've ever seen."

"True." Steven held up his hand and looked at the ring. "But opals are brittle and should not be used for a ring. Besides, their luster comes from water trapped inside the crystal, and they can become dull if not kept oiled. But I refuse to oil the stone. I think it will last long enough to suit me. And if it breaks or loses luster, then it joins the ranks of those things that are merely mortal." He looked close at Ed then sighed. "I must study patience. We are much alike, you and I, though I have aged more."

"I'm missing something again. It annoys me to be so dull-witted. You must explain exactly what you mean, Steven, when I'm being so dense."

"It isn't possible to say exactly what I mean. Some knowledge refuses to submit to being put into words without becoming something else." Steven sighed again. "Yes, it is frustrating." They rode the rest of the way to Port Klang in silence.

When they boarded the bus for Kuala Lumpur, Ed brought up the problems in his garment factory. Steven suggested they discuss the matter over dinner in the restaurant of the Mandarin Hotel, near Petaling Street.

At the Kuala Lumpur bus station, Ed caught a taxi to his hotel. After a shower and an hour of relaxing in his room he caught a cab to the Mandarin, where he met Steven in the lobby. "The Omei Restaurant is on the third floor." Steven led Ed to the stairs. "It's called in Malaysia the second floor. A nasty habit taken from the British, I believe." On the first flight of stairs, Steven stumbled twice. "When I am this clumsy," he announced, "I should always take the lift." He exited from the stairwell and led Ed to the elevator.

When he found that the restaurant specialized in Chinese food, Ed started to ask Steven to order, but changed his mind upon seeing items such as "fried squid" and "stewed duck intestine" on the menu.

After a meal of rice, vegetables Ed could not identify, and sweet-and-sour fish, he took out the expense vouchers on which Faisal Menawar had listed the odd items. Steven looked at them with a slight frown, then broke into laughter. "Your factory workers are mostly women."

"Yes."

"And this item is one that had you baffled: 'services of Abdul Bin Asnulhadi, Bomoh.' Is that correct?" Again Ed nodded. "A bomoh," Steven said, "is a spiritual healer, a kind of witch doctor who still commands considerable respect among most Malaysians, be they Malay, Chinese, or Indian."

"Faisal hired a witch doctor?"

"Better to say spiritual healer. Yes. And I suspect what he did was wise, considering the beliefs of the workers." Steven explained that some of the women probably had suffered from bouts of hysteria. "A peculiar habit of the Malays. The women will sometimes scream and fall into a sort of fit. Sometimes they become mildly violent, behaving as if they were possessed—which they believe is what is going on. Afterwards, they remember nothing and are embarrassed. Men are prone to this, too, though they are almost always quite violent, sometimes killing those around them. Fortunately, among men it is a rarity. Your factory, I suspect, has suffered chronically from the problem for some time, else the manager would not have gone to the extreme of having a bomoh sacrifice goats on the premises."

"Sacrifice?" Ed felt bewildered. "Faisal has a degree in business administration from West Texas A&M University. He is a devoted Moslem, not given, I had thought, to such superstition."

"Perhaps he is as you say. Nevertheless he would have to work with the beliefs of those who think themselves possessed. Thus the bomoh and the goats."

"Have you any suggestions?"

"My guess is that Faisal is handling it as well as possible. Usually it is the same women who suffer the hysteria. He could try isolating them from the other workers. And he could try to find ways to make the working environment more pleasant and less stressful. Setting up a lounge, perhaps? A place the workers could relax, and give them several breaks throughout the day. Maybe supply refreshments. Raising their salaries would no doubt help reduce stress."

On parting that night, Steven said, "Go to your factory. If the situation is not as I have guessed, find me at the Sun Wah almost any afternoon, and I will try again."

"I really must pay you a consultation fee."

"We can discuss that later. It is not of importance."

The next day, Ed went to the clothing factory on Ampang street.

27

After spending some time talking with Faisal Menawar, he concluded that Steven's assessment of the problem was accurate. Faisal, as Steven had guessed, had already taken most of the steps to remedy the situation that Steven had recommended, except for raising the salaries of the workers—something he did not have the power to do. Ed told him to begin with a graduated increase based on seniority after giving everyone 50 Malaysian cents per hour raise, across the board. Ed's tour of the factory and dealings with Faisal took just a few hours, and he left feeling he had accomplished what he had come to Malaysia to do.

But Ed felt dissatisfied. He went back to his hotel and spent an hour swimming in the pool. Afterward, he went to the travel agent in the hotel and booked a trip to Tioman island. Back in his room, he called the agent and canceled the trip.

He caught a taxi to Petaling Street and wandered into the Sun Wah. Steven was not there. Ed asked the Burmese smugglers if they had seen him. They frowned and shrugged, managing to communicate that they did not understand the question. The proprietor listened to Ed with a puzzled look. He waved his hands about and spoke in Cantonese.

Ed walked a block farther down the street and paused to look at the displays in a jewelry store specializing in gold and assorted gemstones. What caught his attention was a man's gold ring with an opal similar to the one Steven wore. On impulse, Ed bought the ring, aware that he was paying too much for it, that—as Steven had told him—it was a little risky to wear such a brittle stone in a ring, and that he would have to oil the stone, if he wanted it to keep its luster.

It took almost thirty minutes for the goldsmith to size the ring for him. He waited by looking at the stalls of batik and watches on the edge of the street and telling himself how foolish he had been for buying the ring. Nevertheless, when he put it on, he thought it was the most beautiful thing he had ever seen, and even as he repeated the accusation of having thrown his money away, he was pleased to have the ring on his finger.

He walked back by the Sun Wah and told himself he was a bit

28

put out to find Steven still not in, that he had to settle the obligation of paying the man his consulting fee in order to feel accounts were settled.

Then he became annoyed with himself for the lie. He wasn't put out with Steven; he was disappointed. Tell yourself the truth, Ed, he urged. The truth is that Steven will reject any money for his help. The truth is that something about that man holds a fascination for me. But Why? Ed did not know, nor was he certain the why of it mattered.

Other people he knew had, from time to time, talked of having a close friend, a confidant, a person with whom it was important to spend some time. Ed had always listened to such descriptions of close friendship with a mixture of bafflement and envy. He believed that he was too busy to give time to such a relationship.

When he got back to his room at the Shangri-La, he found his phone's message light on. The man at the front desk told him to call Subang Hospital, that a Dr. Siva had requested he call.

When he got Dr. Siva on the phone, she said, "Mr. Pitt, we had a young Chinese man brought to the emergency receiving center who has no identification on him. But we did find your business card with your Hotel room written on it. Would you mind coming to the hospital to help us identify him?"

"Steven," Ed said. "Is he hurt badly?"

"I am afraid that is the case. A motorcycle accident, I believe. Will you come as soon as is convenient?"

On the way over in the taxi, Ed considered the possibility that Steven would die. The idea was staggering. Death, Steven had pointed out, was always something that happened to someone else. Yes, Ed thought: and always to someone he did not know or care about. He remembered his response to the dying chicken in the killing tong. Why had that scene bothered him so much? he wondered. And why was he thinking about it now? He imagined Steven thrashing about in a barrel, flipping out bits of refuse in his death throes. "Good god," he whispered. Was he cracking up to be thinking such absurd thoughts? He tried to banish the horrifying mental images, to tell himself that

Steven would be okay. After all, hadn't he been in one such accident? And all that happened was that he lost some teeth?

At the Subang Hospital, Ed found Dr. Siva to be a short, attractive woman of Indian descent who spoke with something of a British accent. She did not allow him to see Steven. "He is too bandaged for you to recognize, anyway," she said. "He was wearing this," she set Steven's watch on the counter. "And this," she put the opal ring beside the watch. The stone was shattered and several chips missing. "And here is the card that led me to calling you. Do you know the man?"

"Yes," Ed whispered.

"I beg your pardon?"

Ed cleared his throat. "Yes. His name is Tung Chung Low. Lately he has been going by the name Steven Duck."

"Tung Low." Dr. Siva turned to the record files behind her. She flipped through one drawer, removed a file, and turned back to Ed. "Yes. I remember this case, now. A car accident some five—no, six months ago. Bruises about the head, some teeth knocked out. The worst part was ..." She fell silent.

"The worst part?" Ed prompted.

"Mr. Pitt, how well do you know Mr. Low?"

"He is my closest friend." Ed was startled to hear the phrase come out of his mouth; he started to add "in Kuala Lumpur," but did not. Dr Siva frowned.

"He is in very bad shape now. Likely he will not survive the night. The worst part about the other accident was that during treatment, we discovered Mr. Low had a tumor in his brain. Melanoma, I'm afraid. We guessed he had under a year to live. There was nothing we could do." She looked at Ed and frowned. "Mr. Pitt, I think you should sit down." She came around the counter and took his arm, led him to a chair. "I am so sorry to give you that much bad news all at once."

Ed struggled to find something appropriate to say, then gave up.

"Now that we know who he is," Dr. Siva said, "we can take steps to notify his family. There is no need for you to stay here. Perhaps it would be better if you went back to your hotel and got some rest. Would you like me to provide you with a sedative?"

"No." Ed thought his voice sounded brittle and hollow. "Where may I wait? I want to be here."

"In that lounge." She pointed. As Ed stood up, she added, "There is one more thing. He had this notebook in his shirt pocket. It has your name in it. When searching for clues to his identity, I took the liberty to read it." She handed Ed a small notebook.

"Thanks," he mumbled.

Ed didn't know how long he sat in the waiting room before Dr. Siva returned, but it seemed like hours, maybe days or months. He sat looking at the closed notebook in his hands and at his new opal ring. When he became aware someone was standing before him, it took great effort to look up.

"I am sorry to inform you that Mr. Tung Chung Low has died." Dr. Siva's voice was little more than a whisper.

"It isn't fair," Ed said.

"No." Dr. Siva lifted a hand as if to touch Ed, then stepped back. "I'm sorry. I know the pain of losing a friend." She stood in front of his chair a few more seconds, then turned and left.

Ed opened the notebook. It was rumpled and creased from being carried in a pocket, and most of its pages had been torn out. Only two sheets had writing on them. One said, "Notes concerning Mr. Edward Lincoln Pitt," at the top of the page, followed by: "When trading for false wealth becomes more important than loving the colors of the clown fish and the architecture of coral, it is time to study the grace of the sea snake and the pitiless eyes of the sea urchin."

On the next page, Steven had written, "I do not wish to die, and yet I am grateful to death for restoring me to life." The few remaining pages in the notebook were blank.

Ed read the sentences several times, then walked to the front of the hospital where he called a taxi.

Back in his hotel room, he sat on his bed and reread Steven's notebook. Then he looked at the opal on his ring, and he knew that he would never apply oil to it.

A Man He Had Never Known

Reed took several photographs of the sleeping man from across a dirt road. This, he told himself, was what he had hoped to find: odd behavior of these primitive natives to photograph. He was a little disappointed that the man lay facing the other direction so it was not possible to get a photo of his face. "Do you know that old man, Adnan?" Reed asked.

"Do. Everone in Kampung know everbody." Adnan laughed. "Old man tired. He work hard as rubber tapper. Come to catch bus. Can get sleep in shade of mango tree until bus come. That," he pointed to a log beside the road, "the bus stop."

Reed put his camera back into the case on his belt and took a Malay-English dictionary from a pocket. Under "kampung" he found "a cluster of houses, a hamlet."

The two continued down the jungle road. "Is the shop house we are going to in your kampung?" Reed asked.

"No. It in Muar. Muar a city, not like kampung."

When they reached the row of shop houses, Reed watched Adnan buy onions, ginger root, and an assortment of unidentifiable spices. Adnan had explained that since it was Ramadan and none in the village could eat or drink anything during the hours of sunlight, they did all cooking during the day in preparation for the end of the daily fast. His family, he said, cooked rice and many vegetables during Ramadan. "Family eat papaya, mango, and banana," he added. "Many banana. Like to eat fish. Tonight, rare meal for you. *Rendang* beef."

Adnan led the way back to the kampung, though Reed could see little difference between the supposed city and the hamlet. To him, it all looked like jungle, with an occasional building visible among the lush greenery.

When they got back to the old man, Adnan stopped. "Something wrong, Mr. Reed."

"Just *Reed*. Or *mister* Lockhardt. But never *mister* Reed because that is my first name, even if it sounds like it ought to be a last one."

Adnan shot him a brief look, eyebrows raised. "Man not asleep. He not in shade." Adnan stepped over to the reclining figure. He lay as he had earlier, facing away from the road, his head on one arm. The shade had crept away from him, and he lay in the white tropic sun. His jaw was slack and his mouth open.

Reed saw an ant crawl across his chin and into the open mouth. "That man is dead."

"Yes. We help."

"He is beyond help, Adnan. Let's go on. We don't need to get involved in this matter."

"You wait with Aziz," he gestured toward the corpse. "I go get *penghulu*—Head Man of kampung." Adnan started off.

"I'm going with you. We can report this, if you insist. But we should not get involved. No telling what the authorities would think—maybe they would blame us somehow for the death."

"That *bodoh*," Adnan said, whirling around. "I stay with Aziz, you go get Head Man. Cannot leave him for crows to peck. For dogs."

Reed sighed. "I'll stay. You go get the chief."

"Not chief. Head Man. We be here soon. You no leave." With that, he vanished into the jungle, taking a small path behind the log at the bus stop.

Reed sighed again, then walked to the shady end of the log and sat down. The dead man, he decided, looked like an old tree stump with clothes on, one of those gnarled-looking dark pieces of driftwood with wrinkled bark that he used to sit on while fishing in Taylor's Bayou back in East Texas. Reed tried to imagine this Malaysian stump as a man as a creature who had eaten breakfast that morning, who had shaved, maybe, then gone out to tap some rubber trees.

But he couldn't quite make it. The thing on the ground in front of him was too heavy, too still for his imagination to give any motion to whatsoever. Reed said the word out loud: "death." But it didn't seem to apply to the dark object on the ground any more than it would apply to those cypress logs at the edge of Taylor's Bayou.

Death was something his father had retreated into just a few months before. Yet it had seemed to Reed that the word didn't apply to his father, either. Maybe it applied to that plastic parody of his father in the funeral parlor. Reed's father had not had full lips for years—not since he lost his teeth to periodontitis when Reed was a child. But there was that grotesque thing in the coffin with his father's nose and the mole over one eye and that distinctive hairline. And lips, full lips. When Reed saw those lips, he felt the thing in the box was not his father at all but a monstrous hoax of some sort. And the hoax made him angry.

The feeling was not new. Even before he got the phone call about the death, he felt on some fundamental level that his father had gone away, leaving an incapable, weak old man in his place, a man so enfeebled and crazy that Reed knew his real father was no longer there. For the last several years the old man was alive, Reed had avoided him as much as possible. That old fellow with the oxygen hose strapped to his nose most of the time and who walked with one of those aluminum walkers people in an old folks' home used was someone Reed could not recognize as being in any way related to him.

During his last visit to the old man's house, Reed had little to say to his father. The visit might have been awkward had Gus not been there. Gus always had something to banter about. Breaking one uncomfortable period of silence between Reed and the old man, Gus said, "I swear, Reed, your head isn't shaped anything like your dad's. Same nose, maybe, but that head. Must of been from your mom."

"Longheads," the old man said. "Reed and his mom are the classic longheads. Now me and Gus here, we're roundheads. That sort of thing happens in a family, sometimes. It's the Skywegian blood coming out. Big jaws and long faces." He held one hand below his chin,

35

the other above his head to show the shape. "Skywegian stock for sure, even in people mainly English. Though there were plenty of longheads in England. Roundheads are a gentler people. They eat lots of fruit and vegetables. A little meat, but always well-cooked, and mostly fish and chicken. Roundheads as a rule don't like red meat. Longheads, though, they like their beef, and they don't go so much for fruit and vegetables. Longheads are mainly meat-and-potatoes men, and a fierce bunch they are, let me tell you. More so than the roundheads. There was a war fought once between them, you remember reading about that?"

"A war?" Reed asked. His father had once been a sharp amateur historian, so there was probably something in history he had in mind. Or maybe this was just some kind of a joke.

"Yes. Fought between the roundheads and the longheads. In England, several hundred years ago. Roundheads won, as I recall. When was that, Reed?"

"In the seventeenth century." Reed was convinced that his father was joking. "The Puritans were called *roundheads* because of their preference for short hair. The Cavaliers wore long hair; they were loyal to the king—"

"Not that war, the one between the longheads and the roundheads. Lot of anger stirred up there between the two groups, on account of the shape of their heads and their different ways. Round-heads won because there were more of them, even if they were a touch less civilized and didn't understand the proper use of cannon and muskets and the like. But, like I said, there were so many of them, and they were a stubborn lot. So they eventually won, even if they weren't as mean as the beef-eating longheads."

Reed stared. The crazy old man was serious, dead serious. Reed felt a knot of anger in his stomach and turned away. This was not his father talking.

Adnan returned with two men, one an old fellow bent with arthritis, the other a young man, little more than a boy. The older one knelt and examined the body on the ground. "*Sudah dahulu,*" he said.

Reed heard a quick intake of breath from the younger man. The older man stood, moving with obvious pain in his joints. He issued some instructions in Malay.

"Head Man say me and Othar," Adnan indicated the younger man, "carry Aziz home."

Reed watched as Adnan and Othar turned Aziz over on his back. Adnan took the dead man's shoulders and Othar made an effort to lift the feet. They took a few steps with their burden before Othar released his grip on the corpse. He stood, mute, shaking his head. Adnan went to him, put an arm around Othar's shoulders and spoke in low tones. The Head Man pointed at Reed and said something.

"Head Man say you help," Adnan explained. Startled, Reed stood. This wasn't anywhere near the kind of thing he had bargained for when he hired Adnan to introduce him to village life in rural Malaysia.

When Reed found he had a few days to wait in Malacca for the completion of a shipment of furniture he was buying for an American import firm, he decided to find out what the Malays were like. He wasn't so interested in the city people but in the ones he assumed to be backward and simple, living in the jungle villages. So he had hired Adnan and had gone to the man's home village.

Othar backed away as Reed approached the body. Reed could see the man biting his lower lip, fighting back tears.

At first, carrying the body was not so difficult as Reed had expected, except for the smell. There was a faint odor of excrement along with the smell of soured sweat, though Reed was unsure if the locker-room smell came from his own body or the one he was helping to carry. Mixed with these odors, Reed thought he could detect the faint, sickly-sweet smell of decaying flesh. As they walked the jungle path, Reed became hot and irritated by his discomfort.

Adnan, carrying the heavier end of the body, seemed not to perspire at all, but by the time they got to the clearing around Aziz' house, Reed's shirt was soaked, and he was cursing in silence. He grasped the dead man's legs, just under the knees, and walked with his arms stiff and slightly in front of him, more like, Reed told himself, he was pushing a wheelbarrow than carrying a corpse. Adnan walked backward, holding the dead man's shoulders.

Women gathered around the house, somber-faced and eyes downcast. Small children stared, clutching their mothers' dresses. As Reed and Adnan approached the steps, two men came to help; one took one of the shoulders, the other took a leg from Reed. With one hand freed, Reed wiped the sweat that ran into his eyes, and he sighed.

It was the sound of the sigh that brought Reed out of his awareness of his own discomfort enough to notice the silence.

The last voice he had heard was Adnan informing him that he would help carry the body. Reed glanced at the villagers as they gathered behind him. No one even whispered, not even the children. He heard only the scraping of his own feet on the tile steps, the faint swoosh of the dead man's shirt dragging across the porch, the creak of the wooden floor as they carried Aziz into his home. Somewhere in the trees outside, crows rasped and coughed, and inside the house a geiko barked its rhythmic chuckle.

When Reed's father had died, he had fallen into a clothes closet. It appeared that the old man was straining to lift a photo album from behind some boxes when his heart gave out. Uncle Gus described the scene to Reed, then to Reed's aunt, to the cousins—to anyone who would listen. Reed had heard Gus's story at least five times.

When Gus saw the angle of the old man's head and the way the body lay, he knew there was nothing he could do. So he called an ambulance and waited in the living room.

The paramedics sweated and cursed while getting the body out. "Stand him up, stand him up," one of them said. "Jesus Christ," another shot back, "how did he get in this position? You stand him up." They worked for at least ten minutes, and ended up having to take the closet door off its hinges.

When they got him on a stretcher, they loaded him into the ambulance ("like they were loading lumber," Gus said) and took him to

38

Thompson-Stephens Funeral Home in Port Arthur. Gus went along so he could sign the proper papers. The old man's body was taken to the same funeral home mortuary that his construction company had renovated, years before.

They laid the body on a straw mat in the long hall of the house. Reed stepped back, uncertain what he should do next. More men came into the house. Several began to undress the body; others carried pails of water and strips of cloth from the back of the house.

Reed watched them wash the body. The men performed the ritual somber-faced. The house was silent except for the creak of the floor beneath their knees and the splash of water. Othar stood to one side, looking away, still fighting tears. Adnan and other men patted his back, but no one said a word. When the body was cleansed, the men dressed it in black pants and a long-sleeved black shirt then wrapped an elaborate black sungkit with silver trim around his waist.

The tending of the body reminded Reed of something he had not thought of in years. One summer many years ago while he was home from college, he had worked for his father's company while it was installing mortuary equipment. Reed's job was to hook up the intake and the drain to a heavy-duty garbage disposal unit beneath a sink in the embalming room.

The mortician, a hollow-cheeked fellow who loved telling jokes but seldom laughed, watched Reed's work, keeping a running commentary going about the use of the lab equipment. "We put the body on this stainless steel tray. See the hole in this end? This drains into the sink. We inject embalming fluid into the circulatory system and drain the blood out in the process. The blood runs onto the tray and out this hole. Then we remove the intestines and liver and other organs that decompose so rapidly. We stuff bulk cotton in the body's midsection and sew it back up so it won't look all funny and sunk in when we dress the corpse for display at the funeral."

"What do you do with the organs and intestines?" Reed asked.

"They go down the disposal you are hooking up."

Reed stood in the kampung house half a world away from Port Arthur and remembered how he had hated the thought of body parts being ground up like so much garbage and washed into the sewer system. With a shock that hit him like a physical blow, he realized that Thompson-Stephens Funeral Home had done something similar with parts of his father's body. Perhaps using the same grinder he had installed.

Reed felt weak, and in spite of the heat, his face and hands felt cold. He turned to find a place to sit, stumbled, and kept himself from falling by grabbing the wall. Splinters from the rough-cut boards stung his hands.

Othar and Adnan took his arms, steadying him. Adnan gestured toward the rear of the house. They released him and he followed Othar through the long hall, down some steps into a room with some cooking pots hanging on the wall and out a door to a porch with a cement floor and a corrugated zinc roof.

"You sit here," Othar said. "rest from death. The men will pray in the house when the imam comes." He went back inside.

Reed took a deep breath. He noticed but was not fully aware of the woman sitting on the other chair across the porch. "You helped bring my father home," she said, "when the kampung men were off at work. For that I am grateful."

Reed pushed the heels of his hands into his eyes, trying to banish the image of his father lying on that stainless steel tray, gutted like a fish, his blood dripping into the sink. Then he looked at the woman. She wore the Malay Islamic shawl that covered her hair and neck, reminding Reed of a Roman Catholic nun.

"I am Yani Kamal Bin Aziz," she said.

"Reed. Reed Lockhardt. Sorry about your father."

"Yes. Thank you." Yani's voice cracked and she blinked. "We are not supposed to cry, you see. The *Holy Koran* teaches us that." Her voice dropped to a whisper, "But sometimes it is hard to remain composed."

Reed nodded, remembering he had not shed a single tear at the funeral for the old man that his father had become. But unlike Yani, he had not tried to hold anything in. There had been no grief to hold inside, he remembered.

When Gus had called to try to get Reed to visit his father, just two months before the old man died, Reed said, "It's a long trip from El Paso, Gus. You know that. Besides, in a few months it will be all over anyway, and I'll be forced to come to Port Arthur."

"Don't you want to see the old bugger before he dies?" Gus asked.

Reed had not answered that question, though he acknowledged to himself that he did not want to see the old man again. And he had been angry at Gus for making the suggestion.

"The imam is here," Yani said. "Now the men will pray in the home."

Reed heard the sounds of the men as they began their prayers. He expected Yani to go into the house, but she did not move. "Won't you go to the service?"

"No. It is not for women. Later, the men will go to the mosque and pray again."

Reed listened to the movement inside the house as the men knelt and stood in the ritual of prayer. It reminded him of the rosary service held the evening before his father's funeral.

At first, Reed had been incensed at Gus for turning the funeral into a Roman Catholic affair. The old man had always ridiculed Christianity in general, but he held special contempt for Catholicism. Gus had spent many futile years trying to convert his brother-in-law, starting before the man married his sister and continuing for what? Reed wondered, standing in the back of the funeral chapel where people were saying the rosary, fifty years? It had given the two men something to discuss and argue about in the last ten years when the two lived together. Gus felt it his duty to take care of the old man after Gus's sister had died.

At the close of the service, the priest announced the time of the funeral the next day. Then he said, "As most of you know, the dearly departed Mr. Lockhardt came into the Holy Church just two weeks ago. I heard his first confession and gave him communion. And it was my sad duty to administer extreme unction to him a short time after that. But we can all rejoice that he found his way home before his appointed time ran out."

Reed felt the anger flare, hot yellow anger that had been so close to the surface for the last few months. His father would never have confessed to a priest. Reed was certain of that. That crazy old man might have—but not the father he knew.

After the rosary service, Gus looked sheepish. "I know he did it for me. He waited as long as he could so I wouldn't be hauling him off to Mass and having him prayed over. I know that. But, dammit, his conversion did give me comfort. I feel I have saved him from something really terrible. Try to understand that, Reed. And try not to be so angry."

"I'm not angry at you, Gus."

"I know that." Gus had gripped his arm with surprising power for such an old man. "I know that."

When the men finished their prayers and left the house, Reed asked, "What happens now?"

"Some of the men build a coffin," Yani said. "Some dig a grave."

"You mean there are no professionals to take care of all that?"

"Do you refer to the funeral homes in your country? No. Here in the kampung, we take care of everything ourselves."

"But you know about funeral homes?"

"Yes. I have lived in Austin for the last six years. I'm completing a master's in business administration there. It happens that I came home for the holidays." Her voice faltered. "Home to this."

Reed heard the sound of hammering. The men were, he assumed, already busy building the coffin.

The old man had earned a small fortune as a builder during his productive years, and yet Reed had been called upon to pay for the funeral, to buy the coffin, to get a headstone.

He had known for some time that when death came, he would have to do those things, for there was no one else to do them. Just anticipating such expenses had made Reed angry. "And it isn't the money," he told Gus on the phone that last time Gus called to try to persuade Reed to come for a visit. "It's the way the old man pooped away his money all his life. Even now, he has to live in your home because he has nothing to show for a lifetime of work. He is so goddam incompetent that it's pathetic."

"Reed," Gus said, "he is old. Your father is an old man."

Then, later, when he and Gus went to select a coffin, Reed asked the funeral director to show them "the cheapest coffin you have." Reed was prepared to buy the least expensive one until he saw how Gus responded to it.

"That box looks like an apple crate," Gus said. "I wouldn't bury an enemy in that contraption, much less my best friend."

"It's only four hundred fifty bucks. The next one up is nine hundred."

"I don't care. I don't like it."

Reed examined the coffin. It looked shoddy: the corners not beveled to meet and the top made from cheap particle board. Much of the brown latex had been gobbed on in ugly, broad brush strokes. The nine hundred dollar coffin looked better, but not by much. Reed was repulsed by its harsh, metallic sheen, though Gus seemed happy enough with it. Reed decided to put up the money for the better coffin. But he had felt angry, even as he made the choice.

Yani went into the house; she returned and handed Reed a glass of water. Othar followed her to the porch. "You have met my brother," she said. "Othar, this is Mr. Lockhardt."

"Reed," he said, offering a hand.

"Hello." Othar took Reed's hand, then touched his fingertips to his heart.

"Othar has won a government scholarship to study in the United States, just as I once did."

"May I get you something to eat?" Othar asked.

"Thank you, no. But you two go ahead."

"We cannot eat or drink. It is Ramadan." Yani shook her head. "But we do not mind finding you something to eat."

Reed looked with embarrassment at the glass of water in his hand. He set in on the floor of the porch.

"Adnan said to tell you please forgive him for being away. He is one of those making the coffin," Othar said.

"And now please excuse us," Yani said. "Othar must go to the mosque, and I go to my room to pray. Please rest here, if you wish." She went into the house; Othar went the direction the other men had gone.

Reed sat for a while on the porch, then walked a jungle path, following the sounds of hammering. He found Adnan and another man building the coffin. It was a simple design, but Reed thought it well-braced. The two men assembled the wood with grace and artistry. Adnan acknowledged Reed's presence with a nod but did not pause in his work.

Reed examined the wood that had gone into making the lid. Malaysian rosewood, he decided. He took up a small hand plane, adjusted the blade, and began smoothing the coffin lid, dragging up curls of wood and leaving what he touched as smooth as new furniture. The work reminded Reed of the boat he and his father had once built in the old man's wood shop. His father had insisted on buying the best materials and had taken much pleasure in sanding and smoothing fine oak for the rudder and the keel.

Adnan and the other man glanced at Reed and continued their work in silence.

By the time the coffin was complete, Reed was once again wet with sweat, but this time he didn't notice. Several men who had gathered to watch the work came forward and took the coffin. Reed followed them back to Aziz' house. He held back while they carried in

44

the coffin. Yani came out and stood beside him.

"We go to the cemetery," she said.

Reed was startled. His father had died on a Wednesday, but the funeral had not been held until Saturday. It took time to complete all the plans, to do the paperwork, to notify all the relatives—and it was necessary to give them time to make the trip from various parts of Texas to Port Arthur. Reed himself had come from El Paso, over 700 miles away. But here, it took—Reed glanced at his watch—only about three hours from finding the body to the beginning of the funeral procession.

"Who must go to the grave side?" Reed asked.

"Only those who wish to go," she said. Reed glanced around. It looked to him as if the entire kampung were gathering in front of Aziz' home. "You may come, if you wish," she added.

The bearers brought the coffin from the house. Reed fell in behind the procession. They took a small dirt road that cut through jungle. Reed could hear the sounds of feet treading earth and the occasional cry of a bird. But other than that, Reed heard no sounds at all.

When the procession had left Thompson-Stephens Funeral Home, a police escort the way. Reed and Gus sat in the limo behind the hearse, and behind them were thirty or so cars, all with their lights on. The procession went down Procter Street with a policeman on a motorcycle zipping past once in a while to stop traffic at intersections. The police car and the motorcycles used obnoxious, piercing sirens from time to time. Reed swore at them. "Why do police have to be a part of all this, anyway?" he demanded of Gus.

They turned on Stadium Road. When they crossed Gulfway Drive, they got into some heavy traffic. Some cars pulled over to let them pass, but most drivers did their best to ignore the procession. One driver cut between the hearse and the limo. Reed swore at him. Gus patted Reed's arm. "I don't think that feller even knows he is in the middle of folks going to a funeral," Gus said. The man drove until he got to the road behind the old high school stadium, then turned off. Reed had wanted the police to chase him down and give him a ticket.

At the cemetery, people gathered around the grave and lowered the coffin into it. Reed could smell the fresh earth and the clean odor of grasses and jungle vines that had been cut in the making of the grave. The imam intoned a prayer in Arabic, his voice rising and falling in a cadence that left Reed strangely moved.

Reed had watched with growing agitation the old man's metallic coffin being carried to the grave side. A mound of dirt covered with green outdoor carpet stood beside the grave. The grave itself was covered with a green sheet of some kind, and it was lined with stainless steel framework designed for use in lowering the coffin. Along one road beside the cemetery, a man with a jackhammer broke up the cement road surface, and repair trucks roared their diesel engines. Along the other edge of the cemetery, traffic continued as usual. Reed cursed the man with the jackhammer, the trucks, the traffic going around the cemetery to Jefferson City Shopping Center. His anger had flashed in every direction: at the police for lounging with insolence on their motorcycles by the entrance to the cemetery; at the priest saying words over the coffin, words Reed was sure his father could never accept; at the coffin for being so expensive and so ugly; at Gus for the tears that ran down his cheeks when Reed himself felt so dry, so angry.

The people of the kampung began drifting away. A surprising breeze came up, and behind it a cloud that promised a heavy tropical rain. The air smelled fresh and clean. Reed walked closer to the open grave. One of the villagers began to shovel earth into it. Reed picked up a shovel and joined him.

After the hole was filled, Reed sat on the ground beside the grave. The other man stared at him. Adnan started to go to Reed but stopped when he saw his face. He signaled to the other man to join him. They left the cemetery, glancing back at Reed, who sat weeping beside the grave of a man he had never known.

Shadow Man

Che Mothar Bin Dr. Hazri dropped six coins into the slot machine and pulled the handle. The painted wheels blurred then snapped into place: watermelons, oranges, grapes, and one double bar. Nothing. Exactly what he hoped the day would come to—nothing. But he knew better, for Bayang was upset about something, and he would no doubt demand that Che do some nasty work for him. How nasty this time? Che wondered. And will I do it? The question amused him, and he allowed himself a thin-lipped smile.

Che dropped six more coins into the machine, telling himself even as he did so what a foolish business this was, feeding the magic machine. Magic because of its ability to make your money into its money, always dribbling a few coins back and flashing its lying signs proclaiming how easy it was to win, always taking more than it gave and yet casting some sort of spell over you, compelling you to feed it more coins, for the next play just might ring the bells and flash the lights on the top of the machine to announce you had won really big.

He pulled the handle. Two stars appeared and a return of five coins registered on the win meter. Down only one coin that time, a victory of sorts. As he dropped six more coins into the slot, someone touched his shoulder. He ignored the touch, knowing what he would see if he looked back. Bayang's toady. The wheels spun then chinked into place with a satisfying similarity of colors: three grapes. The win meter added thirty coins, bringing Che's winnings up to nearly half of what he had lost. The toady cleared his throat.

Che turned from the machine, slit his eyes, and looked at the man beside him. "Boss say you come at nine. Say you not be late." The message delivered, the man walked away. Che watched him. A shabby little devil of a Thai, Che thought. Or maybe Filipino. Some Chinese, some Malay, some Indian, and a European or two went into the making of most of Bayang's toadies. Bayang himself revealed mixed racial stock with his Chinese eyes, dark skin, Malay nose, and hair that might be worn by an African. A tangled noodle dish of ancestors. Arab traders who would sell you their brothers' teeth for the right price. Thai head hunters. Maybe some of those fierce fellows from the cannibal islands down south.

But of course, he wasn't the real boss, nor was his name *Bayang*. He registered at the hotel as Abu Segrin Wong, his idea of a joke, Che supposed, that stringing of Malay, Indian and Chinese names into one, combining the three dominate racial groups of Malaysia. No one seemed to know his real name. The toadies who traveled with him called him *boss*; members of the first line on the streets of Kuala Lumpur who had never seen him, referred to him as *orang bayang*, the shadow man. Che didn't call him anything to his face, for he seemed to lack identity in the way he represented the unnamed men with big money, men from Bangkok or maybe Manila, men who would sell you more than their brothers' teeth, more than you needed, more than you asked for.

Six more coins, a pull on the handle, the whirl of colors, a scattering of fruit, and coins gone. Six more. Che fed the machine with a compulsion he hated, and soon he watched only the stubborn win meter, ignoring the spinning disks, for they mattered not at all. Only the red digital readout of the win meter was of importance.

Che had once scorned those who sat at slot machines, back when he studied at the University of Malaya and then at the University of London, where he read law. He courted Lisa then, blond, fair-skinned Lisa who covered her breasts with elegant sweaters, breasts three times larger than any Malay woman's, breasts he once wanted to see and touch with a passion that robbed him of all reason. Later, he came to believe that he married Lisa because it was the only way he could get her to take off her sweater.

Lisa came to Kuala Lumpur with him, and almost without his

noticing it, children dropped from her while he made himself known first as a lawyer then as an official in the ruling Malay political party. Money came with the government post, and a house just off Ampang street, near the International School of Kuala Lumpur where Lisa sent their children, a house as elegant as the homes of the ambassadors from other countries, ambassadors who were his neighbors and party guests and fellow members of the Selangor Club.

Then he stumbled. A minor thing, he thought: a mistake in backing the wrong idea about allocation of Borneo resources, but not so minor from the point of view of some ministers, who netted him with the ISA, the Internal Security Act that allowed the government to imprison without a hearing anyone deemed a threat to the country. The official stand of the government was that he worked with those who would stir racial strife between the ruling Malays and the economically powerful Chinese community. Che went to jail, knowing the charges to be a sham, knowing he would be out in mere weeks, knowing he had too many friends in high places to stay locked up for long. Most government officials of any importance had at one time or another done time under the ISA. It was part of political life for successful Malays.

But the weeks dragged into months, his friends dropped away, and he even heard the rumors that many had noticed how remarkably Chinese he looked. And there was that English wife, they whispered— not a person for a Malay of real importance to be married to, especially when the party leader disliked anything British.

Che put himself on hold, refusing to think much about the world beyond the walls of his cell. Lisa came as often as the government allowed, which wasn't often, and she assured him that his children were fine, that they excelled in school, that there was plenty of money to run the house.

After nearly two years of prison, someone in the government deemed him harmless, and Che got out. But his life seemed to be in shambles. The Malays in power made it clear that if he tried to regain political position, the ISA would be invoked again; his family, he found, lived with no domestic servants because money ran short, and in a matter of months he would lose his house. Lisa had grown larger, her breasts becoming parodies of themselves, and she seemed to sweat most of the time.

Law firms in Kuala Lumpur had no openings for him, so he opened his own practice. Few clients came. He put his house up for sale. Then Bayang came with a distasteful but legitimate offer of business. Bayang represented an organization that supplied cheap domestic help in the form of Filipino women willing to work as amahs in the households of the wealthy in Kuala Lumpur. Che's job would be to secure the proper papers for them to come into the country legally. He didn't like the work, and he knew doing it would mean further alienation from the elite Malay political structure, for there was much official sentiment against bringing foreigners into the Malaysian labor force. But Bayang offered so much money—enough that Che could take his house off the market and, within just a few months, hire several of Bayang's amahs himself.

Then Bayang came with a special case. One Malaysian client wanted an amah who was only 14 years old. He would accept none of the other women Bayang offered, and he was willing to pay a high premium to get the girl.

"He wants her as his personal plaything," Che objected, repulsed by the idea.

"I don't ask customers to write a job description," Bayang said. "They pay, I supply, you make it legal."

"This is different," Che said. Yes, Bayang agreed. Different because the customer offered so much money, most of which would go to Che. Bayang named the amount, and Che sat back in his chair in astonishment.

It seemed like such a small matter, the looping around the law and beyond the law, the tiny lies necessary to get the right papers. Che worked with a name, Maria Alonzo, an abstraction, and hence not a little girl at all. Besides, she would be a woman soon enough. Better, he told himself, to be a woman in Kuala Lumpur than a lost and hungry little girl in Manila.

Bayang's next deal offered more of a problem: eight domestic servants, ages 16 to 19, for a single household in Jahor Baru, just north of Singapore. "Change their ages," Bayang directed. "And use these addresses as places of employment." He gave Che a list of eight different homes in Jahor. "The addresses are real ones, but you must make up names for the families that live there." Then he handed Che an envelope stuffed with cash, and he left.

Che told himself he shouldn't take the case, that he would be aiding in setting up a house of prostitution. But when he counted the money, he knew he would do as Bayang directed. Increasingly Che helped bring women into the country who almost without doubt would be prostitutes, and there were more cases of lying about the ages of little girls, one as young as nine, a child from Bangkok. Che objected to that case, but not with any real conviction.

Bayang announced that he would no longer come to Che's office, that Che would come to see Bayang at an office near the Genting Highlands Hotel whenever summoned for more work.

Che bought a Mercedes and brought more servants to his home (a gate keeper, two yard men, a driver to take his children to school, a night watchman). Lisa seemed unimpressed, but then she wasn't so impressive herself with her spreading figure and tendency to be morose when she wasn't surly. He gave her a tiny budget each month, not near the amount she had before he stumbled on the ISA, for he feared she might grow independent with money available. She often showed him pieces of art and fine furniture for their home, and he always paid for the items. He liked living with luxury, and buying such things kept Lisa quiet.

Then he met Ani in the gambling casino at Genting. A month later, he found himself telling Lisa about her. "She is Malay," he said. "My own culture calls to me."

"You want a divorce? If so, I am certainly willing to discuss terms."

"No."

"I do."

"I don't."

"Then why tell me about your whore?"

The words enraged him. Ani a whore? After an ugly scene in which Che reminded Lisa that she depended on him for money, that she could not leave no matter what, he stormed off to the Selangor Club for a few drinks. Alone in the bar he asked himself why he had told Lisa about Ani. But he had no answer.

Che left walk-in cases that came to his law office in Kuala Lumpur to his assistant, Ros, a bright doormat of a Malay woman just out of law school at the University of Malaya. Che busied himself with one client, Bayang. Paperwork he required amounted to little, so Che had increasing amounts of time for Ani, whom he kept in luxury at Genting Highlands Hotel. Clients began to come into his office in greater numbers. He got some cases he deemed insignificant, ones Ros handled with intelligence, calling upon him to do the courtroom part if the case promised publicity. Some of them got his name in the paper with a frequency that alarmed Bayang but pleased Che.

He found out about the heroin and cocaine on the same weekend Lisa disappeared.

Bayang, who always dealt in cash, handed Che a stack of five hundred ringgit bills. "Count them," Bayang directed. Che counted the bills, staggered by the amount.

"You want me to do something that I cannot do," Che said, fearing that he would not find a way to refuse whatever Bayang wanted.

"Not at all. This is payment for something you have already done." Some of the prostitutes Che had secured papers for, Bayang explained, worked as mules, a few of them even made several trips between Bangkok and Kuala Lumpur to carry China White, high-grade cocaine that got top money from wealthy customers. Some carried heroin for the street users in Kuala Lumpur.

"This is too dangerous," Che objected. "The government kills dealers in dadah. The death penalty is automatic."

Bayang scowled. "Do not lecture me. If anyone is caught, it will be one of the mules or one of our street clerks like those vile men that call themselves 'the Burning Tigers.' None of them knows you or me."

"Still," Che said, "it is beyond me to deal in such matters." He put the stack of bills on Bayang's desk.

"Do you remember Maria Alonzo?" Bayang asked. He opened a drawer in his desk. Che knit his brows. Maria Alonzo—that name seemed familiar, but he couldn't pin it down. "This is only one of several photographs," Bayang handed him an eight-by-ten color photo showing a little girl touching a man in a disgusting way. The girl had only buds for breasts and no pubic hair at all.

Che had always disliked Bayang, but at that moment he hated the man. "You said we deal only in amahs." Che had to work to control his fury.

"To you, Che, I have never made such a claim, for you are intelligent enough to know it to be a lie. Would you like to see other photographs of Maria? I have better ones. And of course there are similar pictures of other young girls you have brought into the country. But I see you take no joy in such matters." He took the photograph from Che's hands. "You are a good lawyer, Che. The best in our organization. You earn your money."

Che understood the implied threat: take the money and accept the fact that he dealt in drugs or face charges of trafficking in children as prostitutes. He had no doubt that Bayang would come up with a way to publicize Che's crimes with no risk to himself at all.

Bayang pushed the stack of ringgit notes back in front of Che then stood and looked out the window so Che would not have to pick up the money while being watched.

Back in his room, he made furious love to Ani, bruising her so she cried out. Then they argued, though later Che could not remember what the disagreement was about. He went to the casino, handed a floor clerk one of Bayang's five hundred ringgit notes and ordered the man to

53

bring him change as he needed it. For the next several hours he sat at a slot machine jerking the lever with such violence that a small crowd gathered. When he decided to leave for Kuala Lumpur and had the clerk gather and cash his coins, he found himself staring dumbly at over one thousand ringgit.

At his home in Kuala Lumpur, the gate keeper did not come out. Annoyed, Che leaned on his horn, then got out and opened the gate himself. Just as he was about to get into the car to drive it to the carport, he glanced at the house and sensed something wrong. He walked to the front door, peering in windows on the way. The house looked empty.

Inside he found his home stripped of everything, furniture, art work, Persian carpet. Everything. He walked through each room, numb, looking at kitchen cabinets standing open and empty, at closets with only a few stray metal hangers in them, at drawers sitting on the floor, and at walls with nails on them where paintings had hung.

Lisa took everything, he told himself, and he sat on the floor of his bedroom and cried. Loss of Lisa and his children and the house full of art and furniture seemed too great to bear, or it seemed so for the time he covered his face with his hands, feeling hot tears run between his fingers.

But when he drove away from the house, he felt more anger than anything else. How could Lisa do such a thing to him, especially when he was still reeling from the discovery that he had been involved in drug deals, when his financial world seemed to be turning into a nightmare? He needed the comfort and stability of his home and family at such a time, and it felt so unfair of Lisa to deny him what he needed. He drove his Mercedes through the streets of Kuala Lumpur, his fury growing. In his imagination he saw Lisa standing before him, fat and insolent, and he imagined striking her with his fists. Hard.

At the Selangor Club, he calmed himself over a gin and tonic. There would be more time, he had told himself, for Ani, for playing in the casino, for lounging around the Club.

Che dropped in six more coins and pulled the lever. Lisa had seemed to drift into his life and then out, as had the children, as had Ani and Celia Hong and Nor Habib and Waneta Krishnan. The win meter jumped by thirty coins and Che glanced down to see what did it. Lemons. He made a quick calculation, estimating he had lost only sixty ringgit since sitting down. Not bad. A glance at his watch told him he still had time to gamble and even eat a meal before reporting to Bayang.

If Bayang asks me to commit even greater crimes, he told himself, this time I will say *no*. As he picked up six more coins to drop into the machine, he noted that the copper-nickel alloy from the coins had blackened his fingers.

An Odor of Durian

When Cheong Lee Chin picked up the mortal remains of Jude Peckenworth, they were still warm. Startled and more than a little uneasy about the matter, he dropped the box on the counter and looked at the clerk.

"Hot?" the clerk asked, not bothering to mask his amusement.

"Warm," Lee said. He wiped his palms on his pants.

"You not worry." the clerk patted the box. "Nobody home." He chuckled at his joke, then seemed to grow serious or perhaps annoyed by Lee's lack of appreciation of fine wit. "You Chinese," he said, "and not superstitious American Christian, right? You know this just trash, just box with ashes. You know that?"

"I know," Lee sighed. "It's just that I didn't expect him, uh, it to be still warm." He wiped his palms again and eyed the cardboard box on the counter.

"You take to Miss Jackie, she maybe put ash in golden vase, put vase in glass cabinet with red prayer rug on floor in front of Mr. Jude. She think maybe he still alive in ash in golden vase, yes?"

"I don't know." Lee picked up the box again. As he turned to leave the crematorium, the clerk continued talking:

"Chinese not burn body like barbarian. Hindu burn, but even Hindu know ash just dirt, not keep, not want. American? Bah. American Lady think spirit stay by ash, live in golden vase—"

Lee stepped into the street, aware that the clerk continued to talk. He looked back through the glass door and could see the man's mouth moving, his finger punching the counter to emphasize his observations, his eyes fixed on Lee in the assumption that Lee could still hear in spite of the traffic noise and the calls of fruit hawkers.

What would Miss Jackie do with the ashes? Lee wondered. He

looked down the street for a cab and thought of walking the few blocks where he was to meet her at the train station. A glance at his watch told him that he didn't have time to walk. Miss Jackie had been most explicit about when he needed to arrive.

Several taxis wound their way through the peddlers who crowded out from the sidewalk toward the center of Petaling Street. Lee stepped out of the shade of the building into the tropic sun, feeling it hit him like a slap, and all thought of walking vaporized in the mid-morning heat. He waved at a cab.

In front of the train station, Lee paused a moment to look with appreciation at the minarets on top of the building. He had seen them, off and on, all of his life, and he found the building to be the most beautiful structure he had ever seen.

Every time he had returned to Kuala Lumpur at the end of a school year in England, he saw the train station on the drive from the airport to his parents' home, and he came to associate the minarets and spires with all the magic spirit of homecoming. As an adult, he considered going inside only once, and he rejected the idea. The inside of the building, he had heard, stank of diesel and hot bodies, for trains pulled into the center of the huge structure, and many poor and unwashed laborers rode the trains. Lee did not want to spoil his positive vision of the building by having to experience the ugliness inside.

Convinced he stood on the brink of a loss of some kind, he walked into the main entrance.

Lee shifted the balance of the box so he could hold it in one hand and use the other to pull the formal invitation from his shirt pocket. "You Are Invited to a Memorial Service," it said, "in Honor of the Memory of my Beloved Husband." It went on to give the particulars of day and time, explaining the event would take place on the first-class coaches of the train to Butterworth. Such activities had seemed odd to Lee, who had worked for the Peckenworths for only two months when Jude died of a heart attack. But after Miss Jackie explained about

57

wanting an up-beat ceremony for those who loved Jude, Lee under-stood better—especially when she said the service would take place while the bereaved were traveling through the Malaysian countryside that Jude had come to love so much.

Not that Lee had much choice in attending the function. As private pilot for the Peckenworths, he might be the highest paid and most respected of their servants, but he was a servant nonetheless. He consulted the invitation for information on what train to board, found the right one, and entered the first-class section. A conductor scruti-nized his invitation at the door. On the way he had noted with some relief that the interior of the station wasn't as ugly or smelly as he had heard.

He found Miss Jackie waiting for him inside the passenger car. She clutched a black handkerchief, twisting it with a violence that Lee thought would damage the silk. "Is this my dear, dear Jude?" She looked with mournful eyes at the cardboard box. About twenty people sat in the car, and all appeared stricken by the scene before them: Jackie the grieving widow coming up to Lee, who held what remained of her husband. "Bring him here, to his favorite spot in the train."

She turned and walked to the center of the car where she pointed to a seat by a window. On the back cushion hung a painting of Jude. Lee recognized it as one taken from the front hallway of the Peckenworth home. In it, Jude wore a flashy Malaysian batik shirt and peered out from the canvas with eyes that seemed to announce he was about to tell a joke of some sort. "Put him there, for now." Lee set the box in front of the portrait. Miss Jackie made a show of straightening the box, then stood up and spoke to the others in the car. "I shall now tell the con-ductor that the train will get under way, now that our guest of honor has arrived. And, please, do not be depressed by this trip. It is a celebra-tion, the last ride of Jude Peckenworth, a rite of passage for him. And perhaps for others here as well. He is with us in spirit, and I know he is enjoying the party in his honor. We will now go to the dining car for refreshments." She waved her hand toward the back.

Lee nodded his approval. He had been to a memorial service once, in England, where the family and friends listened to a depressing speech by a preacher, and everyone blubbered in a most undignified way. Miss Jackie might be doing something unusual, Lee decided, even for an American; but she honored her husband with dignity and love. Lee felt a tightness in his throat and swallowed hard, blinking back tears. It was an honor to be part of such a dignified household.

As the guests filed out, Lee watched Miss Jackie go to various of the slower ones, touch them and speak in low tones. He had the feeling that she orchestrated their movements, driving them before her as he had seen shepherds bunch and move their sheep in the English countryside. She turned to him with a smile that seemed a bit too perfect and said, "Oh, Lee, you may join us, if you wish." Without waiting for an answer, she turned toward the dining car.

Lee understood her message: he should stay in the passenger car, should be unobtrusive. She had hired him to fly her and Jude from place to place in the Peckenworth Lear jet. He understood and accepted his position as both hired hand and as an ornament in the Peckenworth household, unlike a servant such as an amah, which anyone could afford. Amahs served and stayed as invisible as possible. Lee knew he must be present, charming, and cultivated, should any of her guests chose to notice him. Otherwise, he should be present and silent.

It was an excellent arrangement, from Lee's perspective. He served the Peckenworths with loyalty and without question. In return, they paid him well and accorded him both respect and dignity.

As Lee sat down, another guest entered, a beautiful woman with fiery dyed hair and Eurasian features. *Ravie*, Lee thought, frowning. Miss Jackie would not be pleased to see her. Lee admitted he wasn't happy to see her, either. She would jar the ceremonies, perhaps cheapen in some way the fine sentiment Miss Jackie wished to express. Ravie was rumored to be Jude's lover.

Lee had heard that rumor from Miss Jackie herself just a month before on a working vacation the Peckenworths took to Bali. Lee flew

Miss Jackie, Jude, and his personal secretary, Ravie, to the island, and at Miss Jackie's insistence Lee took a bungalow near hers at the Kuta Beach Hotel. Lee worried that the accommodations as Miss Jackie arranged them meant she was about to expand his job description to include intimacy upon demand. He had, after all, worked for the Peckenworths for such a short time that he was still in the process of learning what they expected of him.

But the worries came to nothing. She wanted someone to talk with by the pool and on the beach during the day while Jude continued to run his financial empire from his room, with the help of his secretary. "Some people think they are lovers," Miss Jackie had commented, stretching her body into the sun, pulling here and there at her swim suit to make sure it covered her properly. "You will hear that. But pay no attention. I can assure you that Jude has no energy of that kind left to hand about to the likes of Ravie, even if he were so inclined. Every night we mate like rabbits, and we sleep like spoons."

Lee heard the rumors, later, and he wondered about them, giving them no real credence since Miss Jackie seemed so dedicated to Jude. In spite of her confidence in her marriage, Miss Jackie kept a cool distance from Ravie. Lee knew Ravie was out of line in boarding that train.

She smiled, flashing her beauty at Lee with a controlling smile, a pleased smile that seemed to have a bit of meanness in it. "My timing was perfect," she said, sliding into the seat beside him. "Hello, Lee."

"Miss Jackie won't be pleased."

"How true, how utterly true." She laughed. "But you must not call the Cobra Woman *Miss Jackie,* Lee, even if she demands it. You are worth a hundred of her. A thousand. Call her Jack. Her father calls her that, did you know? *Jack.*" She laughed again, a harsh unpleasant and humorless sound. "He wanted a boy, Jude told me. And he got her, can you imagine? Calling her a boy's name all her life, a constant reminder that she should have been born a man. How sad. I feel sorry for her, actually." Her intonation betrayed not the slightest bit of sympathy.

"The Cobra Woman?"

"Yes. Yes." The train lurched and began to move from the darkened, cavernous warmth of the interior of the station into the brilliance of the Kuala Lumpur sun, the wheels setting up the smack-smack-smack sounds of crossing joints in the tracks, light flooding over the train, while the lead car issued an almost human cry from the train whistle. Lee blinked at the shaft of light stabbing through the window beside him, wincing as if it struck him a sharp blow. "Doesn't she remind you of a cobra?" Ravie demanded, "I mean literally. Think about it."

"She isn't exactly thin, like a snake."

"No, no. The eyes. Pitiless and predatory. You don't see it do you? No matter. I see it, but then different people have always reminded me of various kinds of animals." She turned in her seat, looking at the rear door. "They're all in the dining car, right? You watch, when they file back in, just watch. It will be a whole zoo. I'm sure I know most of the people Jack invited. Animals, all of them."

"And me? What kind of animal am I?" Lee found himself enjoying Ravie, though he felt a vague disloyalty to Miss Jackie for doing so. And he distrusted Ravie.

"Why, Lee, you aren't an animal at all. Likely you're the only man on the entire train—although, of course, in appearance you do remind me some of one of my favorite animals. In a good way, you understand."

The guests began coming back into the car, carrying drinks and snack foods. Lee turned to watch for Miss Jackie. When she entered, she still wore her social smile. She walked in the midst of a group of people, speaking in low tones, nodding and patting various guests. Then she saw Ravie.

Her smile seemed to freeze on her mouth while her brows knit. She gave several more people pats on their arms, excusing herself, and strode up to Ravie and Lee. "How did you get in without an invitation?" Miss Jackie kept her voice soft, a mere hiss through her teeth. She held her posed smile, but her eyes gave away her anger; they kept darting back toward the guests. "I sent them only to friends, and the conductor had strict orders to admit no one without an invitation."

Ravie smiled. "That awful little slip of paper advertising the train ride as a funeral, you mean? Why Jack, they were abundant and easy to get. A number of people found them amusing and handed them about as curiosities."

"Liar. You will get off at the next town."

"The train runs express, all the way through to Butterworth. Didn't you read the invitation? No stops. And even if you managed to get the train stopped—as I'm sure you could—you would have to put up with a nasty scene to get me off."

"Stay, then, but I warn you ..." her voice trailed off. "Lee, when we reach the tin mines, you will join me and Jude." She turned away.

"Did you see the eyes? And that thin little sharp tongue flickering about? A cobra, for sure."

Lee could see the controlled fury in Ravie's eyes, in the way she waved her hands about, in the set of her jaw. How could he ever have found her beautiful, he wondered.

"And those others," Ravie continued. "Look at them. Domesticated animals, each one of them. That large lady? The circus elephant. And the man with his nose up in the air and brows raised? That man is an American professor on a Fulbright at the University of Malaya. Camel. Trained to do amusing tricks. Back there, the dark little guys with the round, flat hats? Trained monkeys. The one Jack is patting on the arm is the clown's dog. Look at that snout and the way he defers to her in a groveling, canine way. The whole circus is here, except for the lions, who roared with laughter at the funeral invitation and refused to come to the show."

Ravie settled back in her seat and closed her eyes. "And you?" Lee asked. "I mean when you look in a mirror."

"Leopard." Her eyes snapped open, fixing on nothing. "Strictly for show. Untamable, but always kept in a cage." She sat up with an abruptness that startled Lee. "The tin mines? That's what she said. My god, but it is becoming clear. She hates Jude even more than I thought."

"No," Lee said with certainty, "she loves him."

"Sure. Sure. And she told you all about it, no doubt. Did she give you that line about mating like rabbits? That one is a favorite of hers. And sleeping like spoons? I've heard her say that dozens of times. Never in the presence of Jude, you understand. The Cobra Woman is incapable of snuggling up to anything. She hates sex. That's why Jude needed outside activity. Not just with me, either. There were others, I never had any illusions about that. He loved me, though, in his own way, and I will feel the loss of his going. Maybe that's why I'm here."

"And to tweak Miss Jackie."

"Don't call her that. Yes, maybe to do that, too. Did you know Jude hated trains? Hated them. So dear old Jack arranged his last ride on a train. She can do that, now that he is nothing but ash. He hated the thought of cremation, too—which is why she did it to him. The ash is back there, isn't it? That's what she meant by your joining her and Jude?"

"Yes. She had me bring the box from the crematorium."

"There it is, then. One insult after another. She believes his spirit will hang around those ashes. Jude told me some about her weird religion, if you can call it that. Reincarnation. Spirits moving from life to life, always a little lost and confused at death, so they stick by what's left of the body, sometimes for weeks before understanding that they must move on, get another body. Something like the tripe my mother used to try to get me to believe when I was a kid."

"And you never believed any of it?"

"I don't know. Probably not. Look," she pointed out the window, "the beginning of the tin mines. You have a job to do, Mr. Lee."

When he got to the seat where he left the box, Lee paused. "The tin mines, Miss Jackie," he said.

She looked up from her conversation with the man in the seat behind her and smiled. "Yes. It is time. Lee, open that window and scatter the ashes across the countryside that Jude loved so much."

63

"But," Lee began, then clamped his lips into a straight line. He moved to the window and examined it. Jude had detested the tin mines of Malaysia. He had often pointed them out to Lee as they flew over the scarred landscape. "Look at that," Jude would say. "Jungle for a hundred and thirty four million years, and we come along with our shovels and trucks and turn it into a wasteland. Nothing of any consequence will grow there for thousands of years." And he was right, Lee knew. Mining turned the land inside out, for kilometer after kilometer, leaving sick-looking white mounds and white, lifeless holes in the landscape.

A screw holding an aluminum bar sealed the window. "Hurry," Miss Jackie said.

Before we get out of the tin mines, Lee thought. But what does it matter? This is a meaningless ceremony, for Jude anyway, who has gone. It would be just a scattering of ashes. Lee took out a pocket knife and worked on the screws, finding them easy to remove.

As he raised the window, Miss Jackie perched on the edge of the seat beside him, her hands folded in her lap. Hot, moist air poured in the window. "Now," she commanded, "put Jude out, all of him."

Lee pulled open the top of the box. To his surprise, he found a sealed black plastic bag inside.

"Hurry. We're passing the mines." Miss Jackie's voice had a note of urgency in it. She leaned toward him, crowding close to the window. Lee sliced a gash in the plastic and lifted the box. "All of it, right now. Throw it all out. Look, we are coming to the end of the mines."

In a single, quick motion, Lee swung the box to the edge of the window and emptied its contents just as a gust of wind puffed in, blowing a cloud of ash all over Miss Jackie.

She shrieked and leaped to her feet, brushing at her clothes. "Get off," she screamed, "get off me you filthy old man."

The funeral guests stared, round-mouthed, and Ravie issued a piercing, high-pitched giggle.

A scream from the train's whistle cut off the sound of Ravie's laughter, and the cars clanked together as the train's brakes engaged. Lee looked out the window, as did everyone else in the car—except for Jackie, who continued to brush her dress and mutter. Lee noted that the train was climbing an incline, which explained why it seemed to be slowing more than he thought the brakes could manage. The whistle seemed to grow frantic, then became somewhat muffled. Lee put his head out the window to look ahead and caught a glimpse of the front of the train entering a tunnel. The thought of the train crashing to a sudden stop caused him to pull his head back inside.

Just as did so, the train hit something and jerked several times in the process of coming to a halt. The first jerk flipped Lee over the seat back in front of him and the second slammed him onto the floor. He lay dazed, aware that others in the car had been tossed about, and he wondered if anyone had been hurt.

He climbed to his feet and looked around. People were scattered around, most of them on the floor between seats. The only other person standing was Ravie, who came down the aisle toward him. "Lee?" She took his hand, "are you all right?"

He nodded and looked back at Miss Jackie. She sat on the floor between seats, holding one hand over her face while the other made little sweeping motions on her breast. Lee felt a surge of anger at her and wanted more than anything else to get away, to not see her response to the ashes of Jude. "Let's get out of here, right now."

Ravie squeezed his hand and nodded. He took one more look at Jackie. "Her face is bleeding." Guilt washed over him for choosing Ravie at such a moment. He shook Ravie's hand from his.

She looked pained. "Okay, I'll check. For your sake, though, not hers." She stepped back, bent over Jackie and lifted her head by taking her hair in hand. "You all right?" she demanded, and without waiting for a response, she dropped Jackie's head, stood and reported: "She's fine. Maybe not exactly fine, but okay. Only a nose bleed. Come on." She took Lee's hand again.

They almost ran out of the train. Lee looked several cars ahead to where train disappeared into a tunnel. One set of train wheels seemed to have jumped track, but he couldn't be sure. He stood in the sun, staring at the train, trying without success to peer into the darkness ahead.

"Come on," Ravie pulled his hand. "We'll melt into puddles in this sun." He followed her up a small embankment into the shade of a durian tree.

"Jude did that, Lee," Ravie said.

"Wrecked the train, you mean?"

"Maybe that, too. The box of ash jumping all over Jack. It was Jude."

"The ashes of Jude, you mean. The wind did it. I was right there, Ravie. It was wind. Nothing else. Don't tell me you rushed out of there just to get away from a ghost."

Ravie laughed. "Not entirely. You dragged me out, remember?"

He took a deep breath, becoming conscious of the odor that permeated the air, something that he had noticed on some level, for he had his hand on his nose. "That smell."

Ravie looked above them. "An odor of Durian. The fruit are ripe. They have the same odor as human sexual activity."

"People say that. I'm not so sure."

"It's true. Take it from an expert."

He glanced at her, startled. Is this, he wondered, what I chose?

Ravie looked down the embankment. "Thanks for hauling me out of there. I needed to get away from that crazy woman and her herd of domesticated animals that pass for her friends. Look." She pointed. Lee followed her gesture and watched several people stumble out of the train. "The Elephant Lady. The trained monkeys. The Cobra Woman. Look at them—all the circus animals driven out of their cage by a failure of air conditioning. It will be unbearably hot in that car in a matter of minutes."

Lee and Ravie watched Jackie dab a handkerchief to her nose with one hand and brush her dress with the other. "She lied," Lee said more to himself than to Ravie. "Jackie lied to me. No mating like rabbits. No sleeping like spoons. No love and no dignity and no honor, just lies, lies, even in the face of death."

"That is the case, just as I told you." Ravie smiled, keeping her eyes on Jackie.

Lee looked at Ravie, focusing on the cruelty in her smile, feeling disgust for the pettiness of her victory. At that moment he hated her, and he hated himself for the choice he had made.

The Eyes of the Cat

The rain came in a gray mist. Sensitivity ferns along the ground closed so often from the plash of occasional drops that they lay half-opened, energyless, unable to move. My drive home from the jungle's edge took me by a sign warning of a 500 ringgit fine for dumping trash, by a goat nuzzling through a heap of plastic garbage bags, rusting cans, cardboard boxes limp from rain, and rotting fruit. A crow stood on the back of the goat. All of Shah Alam smelled of decaying vegetation.

Danila would not be waiting, not today, not ever again, to greet me through the fence with her passionate black eyes that could hold mine so steady, burning with the mystery of a love I knew was there. I'd seen it, felt it like an electric field, the very air between us charged and snapping with energy emanating from her entire being and mine in the meeting of our eyes, the touching of our hands through the iron gate. She held that steady gaze with me yearning to offer her all the ethereal poetry of my being, to embrace her, pull back the Malay Islamic head covering, take rich black strands of hair between my fingers while her head tilted back, her lips parting, ready, wanting the kiss we never shared.

But, of course, I never saw her hair. It was forbidden. Her body, tiny almost like a child's, brown, I imagined, in the same rich, copper brown as her face, as her hands, remained for all my fantasies a mystery. Danila enshrouded herself in dresses that hid even her ankles, and her head covering wrapped her face like the habit of a nun. She saves the beauty of her throat and breasts for the man she marries. Not me, she said. Not me. A marriage to an unbeliever would shake the fabric of social order in Shah Alam, in Malaysia, in all of the Islamic world.

Danila kept her hands covered with black gloves. I saw them only once, and that at twilight with her looking over her shoulder before stripping her hands nude to brush fingers warm across my cheek. At that moment, the electric air cracked sharp and clean. Her fingers, against me for only a moment, touched all of me with a touch reaching into pain for her words of parting and for the tears, glistening in the last glow of the sun, beneath her almond eyes, her cat eyes perfect and dark beyond all understanding.

When I rented the bungalow on the edge of Shah Alam near where the jungle had only partly conceded to humans, I had no idea what lay beyond the fence around my temporary home. Nor did I care, for my plan was to stay but a short while, venturing into the jungle during the day to collect butterflies native to Malaysia. There the jungle stood, feeding itself with fallen wood and decaying leaf as multitudinous fern, orchid, and tree flashed their green and dying colors into the sun then turned themselves with water into the soil that gave life to other ferns, orchids, and trees. The jungle's feeding upon itself had gone on for more than a hundred million years, undaunted by geologic upheaval or the assault of those massive ice-age glaciers of Asia that never managed to reach so far into the tropic zone.

The flowers of the jungle invented butterflies to aid with rebirth, and butterflies vied with the flowers for color and splendor, besting even orchids and, after aeons, drawing collectors of beauty like myself into the jungles. I came to Shah Alam for beauty, then, and found it unimportant to explore the tamed land, the fenced land of the village. What lay beyond the fence was of no concern of mine, for it was more garden than jungle.

And I came to be alone, to heal from the loss of Julie, who once loved me, whose fiery red hair and even more fiery touch first drove me into poetry when she shared her warmth and body with such intimate energy. For months, my world was Julie, and then she was gone, gone with laughter at my pain and a shrug for the poetry she had called forth with her presence. Her face, once soft in the starlight of a Santa Cruz beach where we consummated our love, her face, surrounded by

Irish-red hair still beautiful there in the harshness of a tavern's neon light, hardened into the cruel laughter of farewell and—worse—into an indifferent lifting of brows when she returned the bound volume of my verse.

Time would heal the wound, I reasoned; time being solitary and the work required to collect such beauty as the Malaysian jungle offered.

From the first, though, I was not alone in the bungalow. There were the geckos, the wall lizards, called *chechaks* by Malaysians for their barking laughter. The tiny reptiles stayed on the walls, feeding, courting, procreating. They called each other with a kissing laugh loud enough to awaken me from the soundest of sleep:

CHEEE-CHAK-CHAK-CHAK-CHAK.

There were black tree ants who perhaps thought of my house as a dead tree and marched along the ceilings and walls in dark lines that looked like living cracks. There were moths that visited through the screenless windows and doors in the evening hours.

There was the family of cats.

The tri-colored mother regarded me as an intruder, for she owned the yard, staking her claim through giving birth to kittens under the bungalow eves, beneath bougainvilleas. An old tom came around from time to time to mark his territory and check on his females. After mother cat gave birth, he dispatched the males of the liter with sudden and feline violence, leaving the females for later use. I did not catch him in an act of such brutality, but saw the results after.

The cats that owned the property were wild—except for the baby kittens, who would suffer me to pet them upon occasion. But soon after their eyes opened, the hissing of the mother and older sister warned them to keep me at some distance.

And there was Danila. She lived beyond the fence in the house hidden among a profusion of tropical fecundity: papaya, banana, cocoa, rambutan, tapioca, mango and starfruit grew in such abundance beyond the fence that I could not even see the palatial house some thirty meters away. I saw her parents from time to time walking the road in front of my house on their way to visit another neighbor. Her mother draped herself in the dark Islamic dress found so often in rural Malaysia, though she would not go so far as to cover her face with a veil, as some religious fundamentalist women did. She was an amiable woman, gregarious and not afraid of speaking to me, if her husband happened to be walking with her. On several occasions, when she met me on the road, she paused to chat, always ending with an affirmation that she would one day invite me to her house to meet her children.

Danila's father drove a Mercedes Benz, and rumor—reported to me by the woman who cleaned my bungalow—had it that he possessed two other wives, complete with their own homes and children. Everyone, said my cleaning woman, called him "Mr. Malay" because of his several wives. It was an interesting bit of gossip, but of no concern of mine. Danila's father held himself upright and stiff, and he always wore a white knitted skull cap declaring the fact that he had once made a pilgrimage to Mecca.

I remained ignorant of Danila's existence until one evening when I went out to look for the baby kittens. For several days, I had seen only one, and I wondered what became of the other two. The housekeeper suggested cobras had eaten them—a possibility since there was an abundance of black cobras in the palm-oil plantation, just a kilometer down the road.

The sky clouded, promising wet-season rain, and the sun neared the horizon. As I looked among oleanders and hibiscus for kittens, the movement of a butterfly caught my eye, a fine wisp of motion and dark color off in the periphery of the yard. Without thought and responding to habit learned during my daily trips into the jungle, I turned toward the butterfly, the lost kittens forgotten.

The insect's flight led me to the fence, a structure of stone and mortar over one meter high and half a meter wide. In an attempt to reclaim its lost land, the jungle had sent creepers and ferns into cracks in the fence, into leaf mold along its top and around its base. Only one gate broke the rigidity of the fence between my house and the estate of Mr. Malay, a black iron gate locked with a padlock the size of my fist and hinges rusted into lumps. The butterfly flew beyond the gate.

At that moment, a blade of light broke through the gathering haze and illuminated the gate and the area beyond it. I had seen such a phenomena several times in the jungle, and the startling beauty of it always caused me to catch my breath: white tropic sun breaking through like stage lights to show a spot of jungle floor in all its wild and profuse vitality. I hurried to the gate to see as much of the jungle light show as possible before mist again veiled the sun.

And that was when I first saw Danila. She stood mere meters beyond the gate, as if in the center of a stage made from a tropic garden, her attention given to a shaft of flowers offered by an orchid nestled in the trunk of a mango tree. She wore an ankle-length, shimmery dress bluer than Julie's eyes, her head hooded by the *mini telekung* of the pious and rural Islamic woman. Black gloves covered her hands, a detail I might have missed had it not been for her posture when I got to the gate, her standing profiled, touching a gloved finger to the end of an orchid blossom.

In that moment, Danila appeared more than human in her beauty, in the religious associations her nun-like hood called forth, in the mystic way she seemed to belong to the jungle garden—perhaps even more than the sprig of orchids before her. I wanted her then, wanted her with greater intensity than I felt when chasing wild butter-flies, wanted her as the focus of the ineffable tenderness her image aroused in me, and I wanted her as a man wants a woman.

She became aware of me standing beside the locked gate and looked my way, first with a kind of almost frightened alarm, then with eyes widened in interest. She gave me a faint smile that made the way she stood in the stray bolt of sun there beside orchid blossoms the most moving sight I had ever experienced, and I found myself grasping the iron gate for support. "You stand in the fire of the holy light," I said, and the words seemed so weak to how I felt. She smiled again, turned, and as vapor once more veiled the sun, casting the area into gloom, she vanished among the plants of her father's garden.

It took me some time to recover, and I stood holding the gate, savoring the experience of the mystery woman's appearing with such drama. When I returned to the bungalow, night had fallen.

The next day, my heart was not in the quest for butterflies; though I encountered rare and beautiful specimens, I lacked the agility and concentration to stalk them with a net. My mind was on Danila, though I did not know her name. It took little effort to conclude her to be one of the daughters of Mr. Malay, but beyond that speculation, I concluded nothing. When evening again came, I went into the yard, seeing only one kitten, noticing for the first time that it seemed lean and underfed.

I had never fed the cats; it had not occurred to me that such wild creatures had need of my nurturing. Cats provide for themselves. Mother hissed and retreated into an oleander hedge; baby kitten hissed and backed away. Its older sister, whom I thought of as *Teenager*, moved back, uncomfortable with my invasion of the yard. Perhaps, I thought, I ought to at least feed the baby.

Such thoughts were fleeting, for my real attention focused upon seeing the beautiful dryad, the woman of Islam and a jungle garden. I went to the iron gate and waited.

She came, appearing from the shadows, and looked at me from a distance of no more than three meters. "You are the American biologist," she observed. It annoyed me that she used such a term as *biologist*, though no doubt it was a mistake she picked up from her mother. Somehow, her mistake—or perhaps just hearing her speak—shattered some of the magic that had surrounded my first encounter with her. The moment of vivid light holding her beside orchids, the moment of her turning to me, composing her fear into a smile was one I had dwelled upon for the entire day. Her words dispelled that image, and I grieved its going.

But I could not regret her presence before me. "I am Sidney."

"Danila." She smiled a tiny smile that somehow blended the reality of her present image with some archetypical figure of perfection deep in my being. The name *Danila* was perfect, the precise term for a woman of mystery, a goddess of nature who was at once someone to worship and a symbol of sexual desire. It helped me not at all to understand how I endowed her with qualities no human possessed, for the attraction of her physical beauty overwhelmed me. She knew of her effect on me, I could see that, and she was moved.

"You are American." She pronounced the sentence like an accusation. "And a Christian?"

I hesitated. My grandfather had been a Baptist preacher, bringing the word of his god to rural folk in Oklahoma. My father spent his life rejecting the god of his father, a god he perceived as being more judging than loving. And I? I gave little thought to such matters, preferring to give my spiritual energy to loving beauty as I found it in the world around me.

"Not a Christian?" Danila's face brightened as she read the indecision on mine.

"No."

"Then you are of Islam?" She drew in her breath and held it. In that gesture I saw both hope and fear.

"No."

"An unbeliever, then." She sighed, her disappointment manifest.

"No. I am not without conviction."

"No, no. It does not matter. Please do not explain. I came because of what you said about my standing in holy fire. You spoke poetry, and poetry and truth are brothers in that both come in beauty. Sometimes poetry is truthful."

Danila's first few words to me could have vanquished my idealization of her: lame comments about the weather or interest in something gross and American such as Disneyland or awkward stumbling with imperfect English to proclaim her desire to practice using my language. But she owned English to perfection, and her

74

understanding of some subtleties of poetry heightened her beauty. At that moment, Danila was the beauty and spirit and perfection of woman, the distillation of purity so often sought by men such as I, but seldom found.

It was for Danila that I had come to Malaysia, though I had no way of knowing until she appeared. I tried to tell her that in the days that followed, during the few moments she allowed us by stealing away from the eyes of her parents and siblings and servants in the waning minutes of day, the short tropic twilight. She warned me that if anyone found out about our meetings, all contact with me would have to cease. She listened to me, her eyes glowing, and from time to time protested that my vision was tainted with intemperance and youth and love.

Yes, I told her. Yes. I was guilty of all of those, especially love, and thus it was that her face, the garden she emerged from, everything I looked upon became more bright, vivid, intense. The universe was a better place for love. How could she not agree with such a vision? She daily moved closer to the iron gate until we stood one evening in the mist and shadows, close enough to feel emanations of each other's body heat.

She put her hand on the gate, and I put mine over her gloved fingers, pressing, fearful that I might be doing something forbidden but incapable of not reaching for some touch. Danila closed her eyes and sighed, and it was then that I pressed into her hand a folded sheet containing a poem her presence had wrung from me.

It was such a slight thing compared to the storm of feeling that gave birth to the words, a mere dozen lines of imagery drawn from jungle orchids to contrast with Danila's real beauty, represented in the lines by associating her with the startling grace and color and motion of the most magnificent of butterflies. She read it, her eyes darting over the sheet with astonishing speed, then looked at me, solemn, through glistening eyes and whispered, "It is beautiful, too beautiful." And she withdrew into the long shadows of the garden.

During my daily forays into the jungle, I spent less energy

stalking butterflies than wandering without a plan, dreaming of Danila, wanting the long hours to move by so I could await at twilight beside the iron gate. At home, I wrote poetry for Danila, though most was unworthy of her. On several occasions, I noticed the cats.

Teenager seemed to grow more gaunt, its ribs to protrude more. Mother seemed thinner, and baby seemed not to grow at all. Once I found baby wailing, uncomfortable, hungrier than a wild animal ought to be. Its eyes gleamed with rheumy slime, repulsive and unhealthy. So I took it the only thing I could find in my refrigerator: a raw egg which I set in a bowl in front of the poor creature. I thought little about the cats, though, my energies being given to the amazing beauty of the moments with Danila.

After I know not how many days of the two of us speaking love in the tiny moments of the evening, pressing hands through her black gloves, and seeing affection in each other's eyes, I became bolder. Though I might climb the ladder of Platonic love, merging of souls comes best in the heat of physical loving. Confident that she wanted complete merging with desperation similar to mine, I took her hand that evening as soon as she put it on the iron gate.

"We are soul-mates," I said. Danila nodded and smiled her small smile that seemed the essence of purity. "We are almost one, you and I. It is the nature of love and loving beauty to share in every way."

Danila's smile vanished, and she looked alarmed, a sign I should have read, a warning that I should not cross certain boundaries. But in my ardor and desire, in the heat of my love, I pushed on, telling her how I had contrived to place a small ladder among the rambutan bushes, just down the fence from our gate, that she could cross the barrier separating us and come into my arms, into my home, into my bed.

Even as I was speaking, Danila began to shake her head and back away. Her answer was to retreat into the garden.

For the first time in many days, she did not come to the iron gate the next day, nor the next. I was in a fever of worry, thinking something must be wrong, for I knew I had read the signs of love in her eyes, in the

76

tilt of her face when she looked at me, in the soft tones of her words, in her words themselves, for she had upon occasion whispered her love for me. She would not miss the evening meeting time unless something had gone wrong. It was possible, I knew, that I had been too forward. But had I not given voice to desires that both of us expressed many times? Wherein could she be offended? Her absence, I thought, came from her father finding out or from her being ill. And if it were not illness, then perhaps she had to have some time to contemplate taking the inevitable step of moving our relationship into greater intensity.

So I walked the road in front of her house, hoping to get a glimpse of her, to solve in some way the mystery of her not coming at twilight through the garden to our special place.

My first walk past the home of Mr. Malay told me nothing. I continued as far as the palm oil plantation, then returned, stealing fruitless glances at the windows and doors of Danila's home. When I neared my bungalow, I met her parents on the road. "Good morning," her mother called out, a sign that she wanted me to stop and visit, which I was more than eager to do. "You must come tomorrow to our home." Danila's father nodded, smiling. "At noon-thirty the festivities for our youngest's daughter's birthday will begin. There will be many guests, many guests. We would be honored to have you."

"Yes, yes," Mr. Malay affirmed. "You will come, of course."

"Of course," I said. "It will be a privilege to come to your home. I trust that all of your children are well and healthy?"

"Quite healthy, all," the mother said. "And all so busy with preparations for the coming festival. Likely it will be a more elaborate party than you would expect. A Malay girl, you see, gets only one birthday party in her whole life, on the occasion of the first anniversary of living in this world. So we make it a big celebration."

Her speech gave me great comfort, for it affirmed Danila and I had not been found out, and it explained why she had not been coming to the gate for the last two evenings. I returned home elated.

Beside my doorway, I saw the cats.

Mother and teenager hissed and slunk into some bushes. Baby did not move, even when I reached to touch her. She growled at my touch, and I was astonished at how feeble she seemed, at how her body seemed to be made of fur stretched tight across bone. One eye was glued shut from mucus. Mother hissed again from the bushes, and baby tried to move away from me, but it fell onto its tummy and was unable to get onto its feet again.

I fed baby a slice of lunch meat, feeling guilty for not having noticed how shrunken it had become from hunger. And I went inside to try writing another poem for Danila. Good poetry had not come to me since giving her the one with the orchid and butterfly imagery, and I was unwilling to give her any inferior writing.

In my elation over knowing the reason for Danila's absence from me, words poured out, many of them the right words, and I became caught in a creative fever that lasted and lasted until I had a poem carved tight from the profusion of words that came at last. It was a good poem, the best I had ever written, and I could hardly wait to share it with Danila. I reasoned that the preparations for tomorrow's party would be complete, and she would come to the iron gate that evening.

When she came, she stood over two meters from the gate. "Danila," I said, "I missed you so intensely only poetry could come close to expressing the void." I held up the sheet with the poem on it.

"Then I must not read it, for your poetry is more beautiful than your spoken words, and perhaps more painful."

"Painful?" I looked at her, realizing only then that she had been weeping.

"Sidney, we must not be intimate. We must not. The forces that hold us apart are powerful beyond my will to act."

I perceived that she felt it necessary to resist my urging us into making love—but the resistance was a mere necessity before giving herself permission. Else why had she come again, why stand before me, eyes red from weeping, to discuss the matter? "Loving is the most natural thing in the entire universe," I said. "It is something that came to us both, unbidden, nor can we will it away."

"Yes." More tears come to her eyes.

"The ladder still stands behind that rambutan bush."

"I cannot. I cannot. I cannot."

"And yet you desire to come to me?"

"It matters not what I want. The force that binds me here is powerful beyond any stone fence or iron lock. It is no less than all of Islam."

"You speak of an internal lock, something that can be opened with the keys within, with love, with desire to further love."

Danila wiped away a tear. "You will not help make this easier, then. Be warned that there are external bonds, too. If the Islamic police knew—as they might well—I know not what would become of you. I would be fined, jailed, and perhaps beaten with a rattan whip. All that binds is not internal. But the most powerful of steel manacles are forged by thought alone." She turned as if to go.

"Do not leave, Danila. I withdraw the suggestion. Stay, share what you can. I will accept anything, anything—so long as you do not withdraw." She turned back to me, and I held up the poem again, offering it.

"We cannot see each other like this again, not ever." She stepped to me, glancing over her shoulder toward the garden between us and her father's home. In a single, graceful motion, she pulled the gloves from her hands and touched the tips of her fingers to my cheek, a gossamer touch but one that I felt through the entire fabric of my being. "Loving you, Sidney, causes me great harm and even greater risk. Risk for me and for you." Tears glistened in her eyes. "I would rather cut off a hand and part with it than give this up, but what I want has little to do with what I must do. Here." She took my hand and pressed a sheet into my palm. There was no mistaking the paper; it was the one on which was written the poem I had given her. "I will see you again, but only briefly and at a distance at tomorrow's celebration, and never again to speak thus of love, never to touch. Please try to understand."

79

"I don't understand."

"Then accept. For me, for us."

She stepped back and stood for an instant in silence as she drew the black gloves over her hands again, an eloquent gesture that said much of the barriers she erected between us.

That night I slept little, dreaming of Danila's dark eyes, of fences and walls and rotan whips. At dawn, I resolved to resume my search for beauty in the jungle.

When I backed out of the driveway, I became aware that I had missed running over baby kitten by millimeters; it had been beside a tire, and it did not move as the car rolled past. Perhaps, I thought, it could not move; perhaps it was still too weak from starvation. Even as I told myself I should go back and find it something to eat, I thought of Danila's parting words and felt the pain of them again, and I drove on, unaware of the landscape in the familiar drive to the jungle's edge.

It was a dreary, dark and overcast day, darker than usual, and I stumbled through the undergrowth, net in hand, like a somnambulant. Sometime during the morning, I saw a flutter of motion hovering over wild primroses, and without finesse, I swung the net as if it were a swatter, slapping a winged creature out of the air. When I found it, I was much pained to see that in a careless snatch at beauty, I had mutilated a butterfly I had long wanted to possess, a green birdwing, beautiful beyond description. It lay in pieces of metallic-green wings scattered across the tops of a clump of bleached primroses.

Near noon, I returned to the car to go home. Beyond all reason and operating solely on what I wanted to happen instead of on genuine possibilities, I hoped to find a way to get Danila aside at the party and somehow convince her to loosen her resolve to turn away.

The jungle, which before was so alive in the misty haze of rainy season, held no charm, and all of Shah Alam on the drive home seemed epitomized by the crow sitting atop the goat beside heaps of refuse.

When the time came for the party, I walked next door. Mr. Malay's house stood among wet vegetation, a gigantic structure with a red tiled roof and arches around all windows and doors. The entire front yard had been covered with a temporary awning by the food caterers, who were busy setting up tables. Inside, Mrs. Malay, whose name I had forgotten, greeted me, showing me to one of only a few chairs in a living room large enough to serve as a dance hall.

For the next hour, I watched a most remarkable and moving display of homage to a child. Norayati, Danila's one-year-old sister sat on a crimson satin pillow placed on the edge of the raised area I assumed served as the family dining room. She wore a long red dress, and her head was bare. Norayati sat in the center of the pillow, dignified, enjoying the attention as a princess might with just a slight lift to her chin and her face solemn.

I looked around for Danila and found her among some fifty women clad in long dresses and hooded nun-like in black. Everyone in the room faced the child on the crimson pillow. Perhaps a hundred people were in the room: old men in Islamic skull caps, boys—some as young as three—in black pants, long sleeved shirts and elegant sonkits with gold threads shot through them, the sonkits wrapping their waists. After I sat down, an imam from the great blue mosque came in. Guests received him with bows and a general moving aside to allow him room near the child. The imam began the chants.

At first, I thought he alone would chant Arabic prayers, much the same way he does in the call to prayer from the mosque. But I was wrong, for soon after he had pronounced "Allah akbar" several times, a chorus of voices joined in what sounded like a responsive reading sung by a choir of Trappist monks. Later, female voices joined.

The ceremony reminded me of others I had seen, in protestant churches, in Roman Catholic masses spoken at midnight of Christmas eve, in Hindu ceremonies I had attended in Kuala Lumpur. Perhaps the most moving thing was how everyone in the room faced the child to pronounce their praise of their god. Norayati remained still, quiet, and composed far longer than I thought possible for one so young.

In a mirror on one wall, I could see the profile of Danila, her face enraptured in her prayer, in her adoration of the divine and of her tiny sister.

After the ceremony, everyone went outside for a meal. The mother carried Norayati everywhere, and she sat across from me, chatting and feeding herself and her baby. We ate rice covered with rendang beef and spicy gravy, fried curry puffs, peppered chicken, a salad of cucumber and red chilies, braised mutton with white pepper sauce, and several other dishes I could not identify, all of them pungent with peppers.

"And how did you find the ceremony, Mr. Sidney?" Danila's mother asked.

"Beautiful. I was moved by the prayers, by the way everyone said to Norayati, 'you are special, and we are glad you are with us in this world.' I congratulate you for conducting such a ceremony, and for having such a lovely daughter." As I pronounced the last words, I glanced at Danila, who sat just down the table from her mother, listening to me while striving to seem indifferent to all conversations around her. "But tell me," I continued, "Is there more to this celebration? Will there be more ritual later?"

Norayati began rubbing her eyes and fretting. "No more," her mother said. "Friends will continue to come here all day, and we will feed them. That is all. Except for the circumcision, of course."

"The what?" I asked, baffled.

"Circumcision. But that is later tonight, after all have gone but the imam, who performs the ceremony with none present but me and my husband."

"But I thought Norayati, I mean I thought a girl was being honored. Is the party for a son, also?"

"No. Those who hold with ancient Islamic ways submit girls to circumcision, also. It is a simple removal of a bit of tissue, the clitoris, I believe you call it. There will be no pain. Some discomfort tonight, perhaps, but my baby will not know anything happened by morning."

I sat in stunned silence. Norayati began whining, and her mother rocked her. "Do, do, uh, all Islamic women undergo such an operation?" I found it difficult to keep my voice under control, but the woman across from me seemed not to notice; she gave most of her attention to Norayati.

"Not all. All from households of the really faithful do. More women should have parties such as this one, and more should have that tiny bit of flesh removed. It can become troublesome, later in life." At that point Norayati began crying, and her mother excused herself, saying she must put her baby to bed for a nap.

I stood, reeling from the casual way that woman talked about butchering her daughter; I felt confused, wanting to get away from that terrible household. After a couple of steps, I stumbled and caught the back of a chair to steady myself. Danila appeared beside me. "Sidney, are you all right? May I be of help somehow?"

"You, you, Danila? Did you have such a party as this?"

"Sidney? Something is wrong?"

"Did you? Did you?"

"Please, speak more softly. I do not remember it for I was so young, but, yes. What troubles you, Sidney?"

"They mutilated you, Danila?" It was too horrible. Hot tears sprang to my eyes. When I looked at her, she seemed different. Maimed. I glanced down at her body, imagining a darkness, a nothingness between her legs, making her less than a woman should be. She followed my glance with her eyes, and a look of understanding came to her.

"You see what was done as a crime." She nudged my arm, leading me toward the front of the yard where there were no people. "You must not. Am I not still Danila? What was done happened years ago, and it was something chosen for me. Do not worry for me, Sidney." She brushed her arm against mine.

I pushed away, not wanting physical contact. "Danila, Danila." I shook my head. "How is it you are so beautiful and yet so incomplete?"

Her face froze and she looked at me as in disbelief, then she turned and walked away.

It took only minutes to walk to my house, but the noise of the party drifted over the banana trees, the mangoes, rambutan and cocoa, across the stone fence. I thought of the ladder placed with such ignorant hope among the rambutan bushes, and I fought back anger. Mr. Malay's party noises rose and fell, muffled by the garden between us; it sounded like such a gay party, but those people were celebrating something monstrous.

As I approached my door, mother kitten and teenager hissed and dived into the bougainvillea, and baby kitten turned its face to me with a weak cry. Its eyes were blind, glued shut from the infected mucus I had seen before. I went into my room and searched a medicine drawer for something to help baby. A tube of anti-bacterial cream warned that it was "not for ophthalmic use," and other bottles of ointment warned not to get the medication into the eyes. Then I found some medicated eye drops, which I took outside and squeezed into the kitten's eyes. It submitted to the treatment, and in a few moments could open its eyes, though it did not look grateful for my help. It hissed and tried to move away from me, but was too weak. I brought out another bowl of raw egg, placed it before the kitten, and started to sit on the driveway beside it when I again became aware of the revelry from next door.

I had to escape the noise, so I went into the house, washed my hands, then went out, got into my car and drove to the edge of the jungle, the place I had sought from half way around the world in order to find beauty.

There was no beauty there that day, for the palmettos drooped with moisture, bamboo sagged earthward, and the air smelled of leaf mold, dank around pools of stagnant water on the jungle floor, pools that were crawling alive with hostile bacteria and corruption. I took a knife and walked into the jungle, attacking it as the British once did to own Malaysia, as the Japanese did when they invaded the peninsula, hacking and pushing my way into darkness cast by primeval jungle.

The sun hung near the horizon when I arrived home. Mother cat and teenager were on the driveway, and at the sound of the car moved aside, leaving baby. But something was bad wrong with baby. I stopped short of the carport to investigate. Baby lay stretched out, its mouth up and teeth showing. Baby's eyes had been squeezed out of its head, like grotesque rubbery marbles, a parody of living eyes. I had crushed the kitten with a car tire when I left the house.

On my way into the house to get a plastic bag, I noticed the eye drops still sitting out where I had left them as a reminder to treat baby's eyes in the evening.

Mother stood beside her dead baby again when I came out. I muttered to myself, affirming that I wished I had not done something so terrible, absolving myself at the same time by saying that the kitten had been too weak to run, to save itself as mother and teenager did when the car moved. I bagged the kitten in clear plastic. Somehow there was no blood on the cat or on the driveway.

On the side of the house, I picked up a shovel, then walked beside the fence some paces from the house, and began digging a grave. As I dug, I kept glancing at the eyes of the cat, remembering my inadequate and infrequent attempts to feed the animal. If I had cared more, if I had given more time to the kitten, bought special food for it, perhaps, given it water, it would have had the energy to jump out of the way of the tire. So it was my fault, after all, I told myself; I am not a nice fellow, at all.

As I set the kitten into the hole, I burst into tears, surprising myself, but unable to control the torrent of grief running hot beneath my ribs. I sat on the ground and cried as a child might.

As I sobered, I became aware of the condition of my clothes: stained with plant juices, ripped here and there, my pants and shirt— the same ones worn a few hours ago to the home of Mr. Malay—were ruined. They had not been designed for jungle-bashing. A small movement caught my attention, and I looked up.

Danila stood on the other side of the iron gate. "How long have you been there?" I asked, not getting up.

"Long enough to recover some respect for you."

"Why are you here?"

"I came in anger. Then I saw you with the kitten and waited. The anger is gone. You wept so hard, Sidney, more than one weeps for cat. You wept for yourself. Not for me or for loss of what you once thought I was. For you." She turned to go, then hesitated, turned back. "I came to tell you, in anger, that you made it easier for me to put our love behind us. But now I can say it without anger. You told me more eloquently even than your poetry could be that we are of different worlds. I knew that in my head, but resisted believing it in my heart." She turned again to go.

"Wait." I groped for words, "Don't go, not yet."

Danila stopped but would not look at me. "You have something to say to me?" She sounded tired, indifferent.

I searched for an answer. "No," I said, and she walked into her father's garden without looking back.

Caught by Memory

Trish Bloodworth was explaining the digestive functions of the stomach when Nor stood up and started screaming.

Students seated close to Nor retreated, staring at her with alarm. Trish noted of the wildness in the girl's eyes, the line of perspiration over her lip, and the trembling in her hands, which Nor held in front of her as if warding off something. "It's okay, Nor." Trish made her voice as soft and soothing as possible. "Nothing is going to hurt you."

As Trish reached out to touch the screaming girl, one of the students in the class warned, "Don't touch her or bad spirit might take you." When Trish touched Nor's arm, the girl's eyes rolled back and she collapsed. Trish caught her and deflected her fall away from the desks.

Nor's closest friend, Siti, knelt beside the unconscious girl. "She get well soon."

Trish's vision blurred for a few seconds and the girl beside Nor's limp body looked like an American girl Trish could not recognize but who seemed familiar. The experience caused Trish to catch her breath. She shook her head, banishing the image of the American girl, forcing herself to focus on the limp figure on the floor.

Trish wanted to remove the *telekung*, the cloth Nor wore around her head and over her neck and shoulders. But there were still boys in the room, and Trish knew removing the wrap would not be well received by any of the Muslims, even Nor, when she recovered. Still, there was that line of perspiration over her lip. Trish had never seen a Malaysian perspire, regardless of the heat.

Nor's eyelids fluttered but remained closed, and her feet twitched. Nothing in Trish's training had prepared her for such a situation. This was no ordinary fainting spell: the girl's body was far from limp. Trish felt that Nor was conscious, though it seemed impossible that the girl could chose to behave in such a fashion.

Teachers from other classes ushered students from the classroom, and three Malay women who worked in the main office came to help Nor. "Miss Trish," one of them said, "you will move so we help girl."

"But I'm a trained paramedic." Even as she spoke, Trish knew that there was nothing she knew to do. She moved aside.

"Girl not need medicine. Need evil spirits removed. We take them from fingers. Toes." One woman sat on the floor and cradled Nor's head in her lap. Others took her hands and jerked on her fingers, as if pulling something from them. They did the same with Nor's toes.

The girl's eyelids stopped fluttering, and her body went limp. "Spirits gone," one woman pronounced.

Nor opened her eyes and flushed in embarrassment. With the help of the women attending her, she stood up. "Did I hurt any one?"

"No. You did nothing to anyone," one of the women said.

Trish expected to resume teaching her health classes, but the principal said the school would close until the next morning in order to prevent the hysteria from spreading to other girls.

So Trish drove to her home in Shah Alam. The whole episode with Nor seemed too weird, too foreign for her to begin to understand. She wondered if she hadn't made a mistake coming to Malaysia, then chided herself. I shouldn't leave, not this time. I should finish my contract. She thought of her record of moving around from school to school, job to job, and knew she might leave Malaysia in spite of telling herself to serve out her contract. She had a tendency to run away when she felt uncomfortable.

There was that odd occurrence of her vision blurring and then seeing the face of the American girl superimposed on that of Siti. The experience caused Trish to feel the kind of unease that often drove her to move to a new city.

Trish decided to jog around the lake near her home earlier than usual, in spite of the afternoon heat. For one thing, she had the park to herself. The obnoxious men who hung around the park in the evening can't take the heat of the day, she thought.

That night she slept little. Dreams kept awakening her, disturbing dreams that made no sense. In one, she had a conversation with a red pickup truck. It was a restored 1952 Chevrolet painted candy-apple red. The truck spoke to her in both English and Russian about a problem in a game of chess. Somehow, Trish understood the Russian.

She awoke trembling and stared into the darkness. That dream ought to be humorous, she thought: but something about it had frightened me.

Later in the night, she dreamed of moving from Port Arthur to Amarillo. Her parents chained her legs and loaded her on the back of a gigantic turtle for a long, hot trip across Texas. She knew it was her fault the family had to move from a place none of them wanted to leave. Something dark and shadowy lurked in the edges of her sight, and her vision blurred. Again she awoke, and again she could make no sense of the dream.

She had, in fact, moved with her family from Port Arthur to Amarillo during her senior year in high school. And she always felt that it was somehow her fault that they moved.

In a dream during the early morning hours, Trish talked with the girl whose face she saw during Nor's bout of hysteria. And she awoke to the sounds of her own screams.

She got up and splashed water on her face. "Get a grip, Trixie," she said aloud. Hearing the word *Trixie* come out of her mouth distressed her almost as much as the dream. It was not a name she had answered to in many years. Back in bed, she ran herself through a relaxation exercise, then, with trepidation she said the word again: "Trixie." A child's name, she thought, something mom would call out the back door at dinner time, and when I heard it, I knew to dust the sand off and leave the sandbox. The raspy leaves of the fig tree would brush her on the deep end of the box, and she would pick up Adalie, her rag doll, on her way into the house for supper.

And *Trixie* was someone who sat at a table in Gates Memorial Public Library, pretending to study geometry while trying to figure out how to get the attention of a boy across the table from her, to get him to say something to her—even to glance up and notice she was there. Who was he? Trish struggled to remember, then gave up.

Trixie was a girl who went to Thomas Jefferson High School, one who was less than pretty and was never asked to school dances. Boys thought her ugly. She knew that because she had heard four of them, the popular boys who played football and ran track, the boys who dated cheerleaders and were elected best this and that for the yearbook, boys with cruel, beautiful faces and hard, compact bodies and cars with chrome pipes and loud stereos—she had heard four of these boys discuss girls one morning before school.

They lounged in their insolent way on bicycle racks used only by boys they called nerds, boys who had pimples and high-water pants and argyle socks and bicycles instead of cars. Trixie stood a short way off. They might have seen her, but it wouldn't have mattered to those boys if they knew she heard.

Lying in her dark bedroom in Shah Alam, half a world and ten years away from that Texas morning, Trish replayed the memory, one forgotten until that moment:

"Some of them gals got flab for boobs like cows, so when they run they flap all over the place, slapping their knees and then their foreheads, slap, slap, slap, slap."

"Jake the jerk don't like the shape of girls."

"Not true. I go for them with firm bodies."

"Like tough Trixie, huh, Jake." This remark resulted in general laughter and punching of arms.

"Trixie is living proof that all blonds are not bombshells. She's flat as a cat on the highway and skinny as a post—she don't even have enough raw material to make a good dirty-leg. I go for gals with curves to them, like Wendy Broussard." He made kissing sounds.

There was more. Trish knew she could recall it right then, if she

90

wished, and in that realization was the painful memory of recalling the conversation many times, hurting many times from the assessment of the popular boys.

But that pain she thrust aside because of the name that came to her: Wendy Broussard. Cheerleader. Cute and short and dark. Big eyes so black you couldn't see the pupils, dark like a cloudy night in Malaysia. Beautiful, popular, intelligent. And Trixie's best friend, Trixie, the epitome of ugly who lacked even the material to make a good dirty-leg, whatever that was. Boys were always asking Wendy for her phone number. Strangers, even. Wendy said it was a bother, but Trixie had her doubts that she would find it something to complain about.

Trish sat up in bed, caught by the memory of Wendy.

It was Wendy's face that had floated before her above the hysterical girl. Wendy: my best friend, perhaps the only one in that entire rotten high school who was ever nice to me. And I had forgotten her until that moment in a nightmare a decade away, a personality away, a name away. Several names, she corrected. Several names.

Trish wondered whatever became of Wendy. They were best friends, weren't they? She remembered walking home from school with her, across Gulfway Drive, down Stadium Road and into their neighborhood a few blocks to the right on Lewis Drive. But she didn't remember saying goodbye to her when her family moved to Amarillo. Had Wendy moved away before that? Trish couldn't remember. And why had she not thought about Wendy for so many years?

Trish fell into an uncomfortable sleep, interrupted only by a few distant glimpses of the candy-apple red chevy truck that was somehow a boy as well as a machine.

The next day in health class, Nor had another bout of hysteria. The students were taking a chapter exam when Nor fell out of her chair and began thrashing around on the floor, kicking chairs, overturning several. Girls gathered around her and chanted a prayer. The boys did their best to ignore her.

Because Nor did no screaming this time, her attack did not

attract the attention of other teachers. By the time Trish got to her, Nor had recovered. She stood with the help of her friends and began picking up and straightening chairs. The attack came and went so fast that everyone, Nor included, managed to finish the exam before the end of the period.

During lunch, Trish found Nor sitting with her best friend, Siti, in the canteen. "Are you feeling better now?" Trish asked.

"Better, yes. Thank you."

"Can you talk about what happened to you?"

Nor looked at Siti. The girls exchanged slight nods. Trish understood; it wasn't easy for these girls to talk to anyone, much less a foreign woman who didn't even keep her neck and hair covered, as did good fundamentalist Islamic girls in rural Malaysia. Nor needed Siti's permission to talk.

"Can," Nor said. "What do you wish to know?"

"What were you saying when you screamed yesterday?"

"I did not know I screamed until Siti told me. I remember nothing."

"Nothing at all? What was the last thing you remember before the attack?"

Nor bit her lower lip, her brow knit. "I saw a figure in white with long hair and a hideous face covered with blood." Her breath became loud and heavy.

"Anything else?"

"Nothing. Only ... only that before seeing the figure in white, everything in front of my eyes was confused, like seeing through running water."

Trish felt the hair on the back of her neck prickle. Blurred vision, she said to herself. The notion of vision blurring brought a wave of fear to Trish, and she found herself holding her eyes open wider than necessary. It was as if she were trying to stop the scene in front of her from distorting, to keep Nor and Siti as they were, crisp and in focus.

Siti nodded. "It was an evil spirit, Miss Trish. Nor's father said the spirit was Tok Ulat. His bomoh told him. His bomoh said Tok Ulat is the evil spirit who lived on the land before the school was built. He wants a kenduri held every year in his honor or he will come back to make more girls hysterical."

Trish knew a *bomoh* was the Malay term for a spiritual healer. The other words were new to her. "Tok Ulat? Kenduri? What do these mean?"

"*Tok* is a title of honor," Siti explained. "A *kenduri* is a feast. We at the school have never heard of Tok Ulat. But we know about Tok Lidah Hitam, the black-tongued spirit. His grave is there," she pointed, "behind the school. But he has never caused us trouble. Perhaps he makes trouble now." Siti turned to Nor. "Did the figure in white have a beard?"

Nor put her head on the table and whined as if in pain, then spoke in an angry tone: "*Hang jangan merepek-lah. Orang perempuan mana ada janggut.*"

"Are you all right?" Trish put a hand on Nor's arm. Nor looked up, her eyes glassy.

"Nor said, 'don't be crazy, a woman doesn't have beard,'" Siti translated.

"I said that?" Nor looked confused. "I do not remember. I got dizzy and everything went black." She looked at her watch. "We must go to class."

Trish sat at the canteen table for a while after Nor and Siti left. This whole thing was crazy. And not just the blacking out and dark visions of Nor. I'm a little crazy, too, getting scared like that—and over what? The idea of vision blurring? That made no sense. As she stood up, she noticed one of the girls had left a notebook on the table. She picked it up, thinking she could return it during class.

That afternoon, during her off period, Trish leafed through the notebook. It contained Nor's notes for the health class, some geometry notes, and several pages of tight handwriting that were not labeled. Some of these passages were in Malay, but most were English.

Trish scanned the notes, hoping to find some clue to the girl's bizarre behavior. Several paragraphs told about how much Nor missed her parents and sisters.

Then Trish read about Othar, a boy in Nor's geometry class. "When Othar looks at me, I know how much I am in love." Trish almost laughed aloud and at the same time felt sorry for Nor. Boys and girls in the school were kept apart. They could talk to each other concerning matters they were studying in class, but out of class, contact of any kind was forbidden.

The school principal had made that matter clear to Trish when he hired her. "Close proximity can interfere with education. It is not considered proper for Islamic youth." So Nor's romance had to rest upon an exchange of glances and carried out in her imagination.

The problem was, though, that Nor could not be sure Othar had ever noticed her. She wrote about the energy she had put into simply getting him to look at her: if he would just look, "I could tell him with my eyes how much I adore him."

When Trish read that statement, her vision blurred. She looked up, trying to focus her eyes on something. Anything. But it was no use, and Trish knew what was coming—images from a memory lost until that moment. But she was not prepared for how vivid the images were or for the intensity of the feelings that came with them.

Paul Newton sat in Gates Memorial Public Library before a massive oak table, muttering into a book and glancing from it to the chess board in front of him. He looked regal, Trixie thought, sitting in a throne-like oak chair.

Trixie had sat across from him in hopes of finding some way to get his attention, of exchanging a few words—it didn't matter what, just so he talked to her. Her heart was beating so hard and her breathing was so shallow that she became faint. She made herself take several deep breaths to steady herself. Paul glanced at her, and she looked down at her geometry book. Even as she did so, she realized that he had not seen her. She looked at him again. The book he held was not in

English—it wasn't even in a normal alphabet. Russian, she decided, with a touch of awe. Paul Newton can read Russian.

How could she get his attention? The chess board, maybe? Her father had taught her the game when she was a child, and he told her she had a gift for it. But she had never played anyone but him. She looked at Paul's board and assessed the situation: mate in two moves, if it was white's turn, three if it was not.

Trixie told him what she thought, pointing out the obvious moves.

And that was the beginning, Trish remembered, and her vision cleared. She stood and went to the windows that ran all the way across the wall opposite the quadrangle. Outside the building was the soccer field the boys used, and beyond that a fence separating the field from the swampy edges of the Klang River. On the other side of the river stood the tangle of trees and vines of the river jungle, green and beautiful beyond words. Among the greenery stood several trees that the students called "Flame of the Forest," covered with fiery orange-red blossoms. Sometimes Trish saw monkeys playing among the brilliant flowers and on the palm fronds along the edge of the jungle.

"Paul Newton," she said, marveling that she had not remembered his name for many years. He had meant so much to her—and she to him. She had been wrong about the moves in that chess game, but that mattered not at all. It gave Paul the opportunity to explain the chess problem as he had found it in the Russian book.

Paul had taught himself enough Russian so he could read the chess books in the library because he had read all the ones it had in English. That was how he was, Trish remembered: if he wanted something, he went after it with a furious intensity, sweeping aside whatever got in his way.

Before long, Paul had wanted Trixie, and she offered no resistance, trusting him in every way. And she got pregnant.

The memory of the pregnancy and the abortion caused Trish to feel dizzy. She scanned the palm fronds for monkeys, but there were none.

Trish felt as if she had opened a long-shut door and was looking into a room full of grotesque and forgotten furniture. Sequence of events didn't matter: at a glance she could see so much. The drive back from Galveston with Paul grim and silent and her feeling so empty, so afraid of having made a mistake, afraid of Paul's silence, of her parents finding out. But there was also the ecstasy in motel rooms and in the bedrooms of her parents' home. Not just physical ecstasy. Spiritual. She felt sure she and Paul were soul-mates, exploring each other and themselves in the intimacy of touch away from the eyes of others, in the bedrooms, in the dark end of town on Procter Street, touching within the cab of his red pickup.

"The pickup in my dream," Trish whispered, standing in her classroom across from the tangled lianes and intense greenery of the Klang river jungle.

What happened to Paul, to the boy who called her pet names, who bought perfume and jewelry for her? She remembered a bracelet he gave her—a silver one that he had engraved with the words "for Kitten from Paul." The bracelet vanished sometime in the past, or she would have found it among her jewelry, and it would have reminded her of that lost era of her life.

What had become of her and Paul? She didn't know. The mental room she opened contained only so many memories.

Had her parents moved to Amarillo to get her away from Paul? They had found out about the trip to Galveston, maybe, and decided it was time to separate the lovers? Somehow that explanation rang hollow to Trish. It wasn't her parents' style to control her so much. Or was it?

And why had her memory played such terrible tricks on her? Hiding Paul from her for so many years, hiding Wendy Broussard. She was certain that they were the only two people in that whole horrible school in Port Arthur who were worth remembering. And yet she had lost them for ten years. Parts of them were still lost.

That night, she calculated the time difference between Shah Alam and Amarillo. It would be 13 hours earlier in her mother's home.

So at nine o'clock, she called, knowing she could catch mom before she left for work.

After initial greetings, Trish got right to the point: "Mom, what was the real reason we moved away from Port Arthur?"

"Your father got a good job at the *Amarillo Globe-News*, don't you remember?

"I remember we had to scrimp, that his income dropped or wouldn't go as far. Maybe the job wasn't that good? Maybe there was another reason for the move? A real reason, not just a good one."

"Your father became City Editor, Trish."

"Yeah, later. Mom, level with me. Did we move because of Paul Newton?" There was a long silence. "Mom?" Trish felt her heart rate increase.

"Who have you been talking to?" Her mother's voice sounded unsteady.

"Nobody. I just remembered him today, remembered that once he was the most important person in my life. As far as I can determine, I had not thought about him for ten years. Don't you think that a bit weird? And I cannot remember what happened to him and me."

"Trish, Trish, Trish." It was something mom said when she was worried. Hearing it caused Trish considerable alarm.

"Mom, I've got to know. And there are some other things, too. My mind has been doing some funny tricks on me. I have always had a good memory. A great memory. It got me a university degree with little effort. And yet, for something as important as Paul Newton, it let me down for ten years."

"Trish, please, let it go. This digging into the past will do you no good, no good at all. Take my word for it."

"I can't do that, and you know it. Suppose you discovered that for the last few years you had completely forgotten about me and Dad?"

"Now, Trish, that's impossible—"

"No, it isn't. Just listen. Suppose you had forgotten about me and Dad, then one day, for no good reason, you remembered giving birth to me and raising me until I was three, and you remembered the life you and Dad shared up until that time. But you couldn't remember what happened beyond that time. No matter how hard you tried, you couldn't recall what became of us. Nothing. Zilch. Wouldn't you be just a little eager to find out? And would you accept the advice from your own mother to leave it alone?"

"Trish, this is a different matter—"

"No different. I have lived for ten years without even thinking about Paul. Or Wendy Broussard, my best friend. Something bad is wrong with me, and you have got to help. Mom? Please stop crying. That doesn't help. Mom?"

"I'm all right."

"You are not. You're crying. Look, I'm sorry this is hard for you. But it's terrible for me. Please, Mom, help me."

"Trish." Mom's voice broke and she took a moment to collect herself. "Trish, I want to help you. But don't ask me about all that. I can't tell you anything."

Trish wavered between anger and concern for her mother. "All right. All right. For now, at any rate, I'll drop it if you will tell me just one thing. Did you take me away from Port Arthur to get me away from Paul?"

"No, Trish, as God is my witness."

The next day, the whole school seemed to go crazy. Nor had another fit of hysteria, this time in the quadrangle. She began with incoherent screams, then attacked a male student, striking him in the head with a rock.

Trish rushed to the window of her class and saw the boy go down. Several other boys dragged him into a building, and girls surrounded the hysterical girl, some chanting prayers. Trish was unsure of what happened next. Most of the other girls in the quadrangle became hysterical, some falling down as in a faint, others screaming. One group moved like a wave of berserkers to the building across from where Trish stood and began breaking windows with bricks they pried up from the walkway. Some picked up pieces of glass, others armed themselves with rocks, and they returned to the center of the quadrangle.

The girls attacked anyone who came into the quadrangle, pelting them with shards of glass and stones. The siege went on for hours.

Trish made her way to the main office and helped turn it into an infirmary. She treated those wounded by the girls in the quadrangle, starting first with the ones who had been cut with window glass. None of them were serious, though one girl had a scalp wound that bled enough to frighten Trish.

While she was stanching the flow from the girl's scalp, Trish felt her vision begin to blur, and for a few seconds, she was looking not at a wounded Malay but at Wendy, and it was Wendy's blood running down her face. "No," Trish commanded. Those in the room looked at Trish, startled, and the girl she was treating jerked back. "Be still," Trish said. "This will hurt just a bit."

Her vision cleared, but Trish knew it was an act of will. This girl needed her worse right then than Trish needed to allow entry to whatever was trying to get through from her past.

When the police arrived, the girls in the quadrangle attacked them, too, and they drew back. By that time, there were reporters on the scene from the *Malay Mail* and the *New Straits Times*.

Nor's father came into the office with a man he introduced as a bomoh. The principal ordered them out, but changed his mind when a reporter argued that the bomoh might be able to help if for no other reason than the girls' believing that he had some power.

The bomoh went into the quadrangle chanting in a deep, resonate voice and weaving patterns in the air with his hands. His presence had a calming effect on the girls. He went to each one and touched her forehead. Trish was astonished by the effect of the bomoh. "What is he doing?"

"Treating them with *air jampi*," the principal said. "It is a kind of medicinal water or spirit water. And he is chanting an incantation he thinks will counter evil."

Within minutes, the bomoh had ended the bout of hysteria. Some of the girls fainted as he treated them with the water, others began wandering out of the quadrangle in a daze. Later, when questioned about their behavior, none remembered anything they did while in the grip of hysteria.

By the time Trish left campus, the bomoh had finished with the girls and was wandering around campus trying, as the principal explained to Trish, to locate the resting place of the evil spirit, Tok Ulat.

When Trish got home, she sat in her living room and made a deliberate effort to banish the images of hysterical girls and the spiritual healer from her mind. Then she tried to recall the memory that nearly broke through while treating the wounded girl. But nothing came. So she gave her attention again to the problems at school, to trying to understand what could cause the girls to behave in such strange ways. She drew a blank there, too, and the uncertainty of it all made her uncomfortable.

Maybe, she thought, she would have to give up on Malaysia, go back to Amarillo, or perhaps look for another foreign job. I could seek employment in a more western environment, like Australia. Yes, and I'd be running away again. How many places have I fled since leaving Amarillo? Five?

That evening, just before dusk, she went for her daily jog around the lake near her house. As usual, there were plenty of what she had come to call "howdy boys" in the park. "Alu, alu, alu," they said as she jogged by. She ignored them, and she was careful not to make eye contact with any of them. If she did, she knew that some of them would make kissy noises at her.

The first time she got the kissy noises directed at her, she had gone home furious, insulted. Later, Dr. Nik Isahak explained that the gesture was not as insulting in Malaysia as it would be in the United States. "They are simply telling you they find you attractive. It is sort of like a wolf whistle—crude but not threatening or obscene." He said that because of her fair skin and long, blond hair, she was the ideal of female beauty in southeast Asia.

Nik was embarrassed, he said, about how some of his fellow Malays treated her. "But I once did similar things," he said, "when I was a young man—before going to England to study medicine. These young men, they have never lived in another culture and so have never learned how crass they are."

The explanation curbed her anger some, but she still hated the attention from the howdy boys.

As she turned to jog across the bridge near one end of the lake, she saw some men wearing rubber diving suits and oxygen bottles, preparing to go into the murky waters. She stopped running. Something about the scene was familiar. Her vision became blurry. "Alu, alu, alu," a Malay boy said as he jogged by.

Trish sat on the grass by the edge of the lake, drew up her knees and covered her face with her hands. The memory that came this time was from the television screen in her home in Port Arthur: men in rubber suits diving under the Rainbow Bridge into the waters of the Neches River.

They pulled up two bodies, both encased in mud. They were Lou Anne Theriot and James Ralston, the news commentator said, seniors in Port Neches High School.

Trixie didn't know them, but there was plenty of talk about them for the next few days at Thomas Jefferson High. The Port Neches school was just down the road, almost a sister high school. The kids who died were popular, if you could believe the gossip. Lovers. Dedicated to each other, said some of the gossips, who loved the excitement, the romantic horror of the suicides. Lou Anne and James were like Romeo and Juliet, the gossips said: when it became clear to them that they could not spend the rest of their lives together, they decided to die together.

They wrote suicide notes, mailed them to their parents, then drove toward Bridge City. On the top of the Rainbow Bridge, the tallest bridge in Texas, James parked his Thunderbird. They got out of the car,

101

climbed over the railing, and—according to motorists who were on the bridge at the time—jumped while holding hands.

The fall separated them, and when they hit the water, they kept going down until their bodies lodged in the mud. It took divers hours to locate them and bring them to the surface.

Trish became aware someone was talking to her. She looked up at a braver-than-usual howdy boy who had broken away from the crowd and come over to her. "What did you say?"

"I said I am Adenan. Can I know you?"

He was about her age, perhaps younger. His skin was flawless, a perfect deep brown, and his face was handsome. She waved a hand, dismissing his question. "What are the divers looking for?"

"Someone said they look for stolen things. Tools. I do not know. Can I know your name?"

"My name is Trish. But that is all I'm willing to tell."

Adenan's face showed his disappointment. "You will not tell your phone number?"

Trish stood up. She was several inches taller than he, a fact that surprised them both. "I give my phone number only to friends." She jogged toward the bridge. Adenan jogged beside her.

"But you know my name. Adenan. And I know you are Trish. Are we not friends, then?" Trish drew her mouth into a sneer, set her eyes into a frown and looked at him. Adenan looked startled and frightened and vanished from her field of vision.

The anger Trish flashed at him was contrived for effect, though she was annoyed that he had come at that moment, the precise time when her memory seemed to be unraveling something important.

But what was so important about Lou Anne and James, she asked herself during her shower. I didn't know them. Sure, it was sad that they had been so stricken with romantic agony that they thought they had no way out of terrible circumstances other than through suicide. But that was over ten years ago, and it happened to strangers. What had their trip up the Rainbow Bridge to do with me? She knew the memory was important or she would not have buried it so deep. And it would not have come leaping to life with such drama.

That night she dreamed of Wendy, who wore the Islamic head covering of Malay women. She came to Trish's house, smashed out a window, and came after Trish with a piece of glass the size of a sword. When she started hacking, Trish was watching from another angle, and the girl being stabbed was Wendy. Furious, hysterical Wendy slashed away at beautiful, defenseless Wendy until Trixie's friend lay in a pool of blood on the floor. Trish awoke to the sound of her own screams.

She got up and turned on a light, a silly gesture, she told herself. But the yellow glow gave her comfort. It affirmed that she was in her Malaysian home with its mosaic rosewood floors and high ceilings, a place she had come to love. She looked around the room to calm herself, then gave her attention to the dream.

So Wendy was dead. The dream had nudged the real memory into consciousness. Trish allowed the image to come in all its horror.

In the second floor hall of Thomas Jefferson High School, after most people had left the building for the day, Wendy had taken a pistol from her purse and fired a bullet into her brain. Trixie heard the shot, and she joked with Paul about it, or had tried to. Paul was sullen, had been since before their trip to Galveston. He seldom laughed, but that didn't stop Trixie from trying to get a smile out of him. "I'll bet somebody set a cherry bomb off in Petunia's classroom," she said. Petunia was the name Paul had given to Miss Michaelson, their English teacher.

They were to meet Wendy by Trixie's locker, and they got there just after Wendy's final act. The dripping, maimed thing they found on the floor bore little resemblance to the vibrant Wendy they knew, and for a few heart-stopping seconds, Trixie thought it might be someone else. But she knew that paisley pattern in the blue dress, and she turned to Paul in wild grief.

Trish paced around her room, accepting the vision of Wendy dead on the floor in the growing pool of blood but refusing to accept the old pain, the intense craziness of it with all its blinding light shattering her vision like looking at the sun. That was for another time, not for today, not for me now, not for the adult Trish, the health teacher in Malaysia.

Was the sight of Wendy what had driven Trish to shut out her memories? It was reasonable to believe so. But she still found holes in the past. Where did Paul go? And what drove her parents to move seven hundred miles across Texas?

Trish went to the kitchen and made coffee. The motorcycle outside her front door told her it was six in the morning, time for the Chinese-Malaysian woman to cycle by and leave the *New Straits Times* hanging on her gate. She could read about the hysteria in her school.

The article, long and detailed, included a photograph of one of the girls chasing a boy with a brick. A total of 24 girls were caught by the hysteria, the article said. And it quoted the bomoh, who claimed the evil spirit Tok Ulat was responsible for the mayhem. The bomoh thought he had cast out the spirit, and he was sure it would have no more power over the girls.

The girls interviewed by the reporter claimed they had no memory of anything after they heard Nor begin screaming.

A week earlier, Trish would have scoffed at such a memory lapse. The girls had, after all, kept everyone at bay for several hours. It wasn't as if they were in a trance or unconscious all that time. Some of them had the presence of mind to be quite accurate in hurling stones and slashing at people with glass. But that day, Trish was ready to believe. Those girls were, in their current state of mind, innocent of what they had done—of that Trish was certain, however unreasonable it might seem to the uninitiated, to those, like Trish a week before, who had no way of knowing first hand the tricks the mind could play.

That morning when Trish got to school, the day's drama had already begun. The girls were in the quadrangle, digging up bricks and knocking out windows. "It is the very same girls," the principal said when Trish went to his office. "That fool bomoh said this would not happen again, and I was absurd enough to believe."

Trish did notice, though, that the principal had been enough of a skeptic to have several new first-aid kits on hand. She complimented him on this, then set to work on the wounded. There were fewer to deal with since most had learned to respect the territory of the berserk girls in the quadrangle.

"I am glad it is only the girls," the principal told her. "If it were the boys, there would be some deaths. In Malaysia, only girls suffer from hysteria, and only boys run amok. It is a Malay word, *amok*, did you know? When a boy or a man runs amok, always someone dies."

Trish knew. She had read it in the newspaper article. But it made no sense that the boys at the school were unaffected. Not that it made much sense that the girls were. Little on campus the last several days made sense.

The police arrived again, and before long, Trish treated one for a cut on his head. The bomoh came again, and again he was able to calm the girls with his baritone chant, his eloquent gestures, and the special water. Again they were embarrassed and contrite, and none of them remembered anything. The principal declared the school closed for the rest of the day, repeating his fear that the hysteria could infect the other girls.

Trish went to her room to gather some books. Tomorrow, she told herself, she just might not show up for work. She picked up Nor's notebook.

That evening, Trish read every English entry Nor had written, but learned little of any use in understanding why the girl behaved as she did. She wrote about how much she loved Othar and about her fear of losing him. In one touching passage, she had written, "I love Othar, and I think it is with all my soul. But he looks the other way. How can I know if this is true love, the kind that lasts forever, or just monkey love?"

Monkey love? Trish laughed at the expression, then looked it up in her book on *bahasa Malaysia*, the Malay language. "Puppy love," it said. "The love experienced by adolescents. Not a lasting love."

The final phrase caught her attention. It sounded like a line from some old popular song. But there was something else about it, too, something that she felt as a dull pain somewhere under her ribs.

"Ours is not a lasting love," she had told Wendy. The memory of the conversation came to Trish as she might remember an event the previous week: vivid and clear and without the distortion of vision that accompanied the arrival of other memories from that hazy past in East Texas.

She had cried when she confessed her fear to Wendy. They were in Wendy's bedroom, a paneled room added to the house by closing off the double garage. Wendy had made the room a showcase of her personality: photographs of her with various friends took up one wall. Posters covered another wall, one a gift from Trixie. It showed a giant goldfish looking into a tiny goldfish bowl in which a kitten was trapped. Wendy had just washed her hair, and Trixie was rolling it in curlers. They talked in soft tones.

"Paul Newton isn't worth a single one of your tears," Wendy told her. "He lacks passion."

"That's not true. My trip to Galveston is proof of that."

"I'm not talking about sex. Anybody can do sex. I'm talking about something else. He never gives himself, not really. He is always sitting there behind those gorgeous blue eyes analyzing everything, like you were a curious game and not a person." Wendy spoke with such intensity that Trixie found herself believing the words.

And for a moment Trixie wondered how Wendy knew those things. Did Wendy and Paul ...? No. She couldn't even complete the question.

Then Trish remembered another conversation in that room. Did it take place that same evening? She couldn't be sure. But the words themselves came to her with painful clarity. Wendy was crying, strong Wendy who had never seemed bothered by anything, beautiful Wendy who seemed to have everything that Trixie did not, had become sad

Wendy in her pouring out a stunning tale.

Wendy's father had begun abusing her when she was only six. He never hurt her physically, and he always seemed gentle and loving. But he abused her nevertheless, and he did so from time to time throughout her life until just a few weeks before when Wendy felt confident enough, brave enough to tell her mother. "I had to, Trixie. I had to tell someone. It was making me crazy. I felt guilty all the time, and I hated myself for what was going on."

Her family was breaking up. Wendy wasn't clear on all the details about how her parents were handling the matter of divorce, but she knew her father had left under the pretext of going on a business trip, then sent word that he was not coming back. "This isn't what I wanted. I love my father. Sometimes I hate him, but I love him. I don't want to be the cause of my parents' divorce."

Trish searched through the care package her mother had sent along with her when she left for Malaysia and found a bottle of Valium. It was something Trish had thought she would never use. But she wanted no dreams that night, and she didn't care if she overslept since she thought she would quit that terrible job, anyway.

Nevertheless, she awoke at her usual time, and she found herself going to school. It would be the last day on that job, she told herself.

When she got to campus, all was calm. The atmosphere seemed quieter than usual, and the students seemed subdued. But then the students on that campus never were a rowdy lot—except when they become hysterical.

Several girls were missing from each of her classes, and by third period, Trish knew had happened. Siti confirmed it by whispering to her before class, "All of the girls who suffered hysteria have been taken out of the school." Siti looked around and lowered her voice even more. "Nor's father says he will move her to Kuala Selangor." Siti's face remained stoic, but tears filled her eyes and spilled down her cheeks.

During her off period, Trish stood at the window and watched the monkeys play in the edge of the river jungle. She considered finishing the day, then telling the principal she would not be back. Or perhaps I ought to give two weeks' notice. That would be the professional thing to do. But it was so tempting just to run, perhaps even to leave right then, get into her car and drive away. She had run out on plenty of other jobs. Since graduating from college, Trish had lived in five cities. With each move, she had changed her first name: she had been Pat, Patsy, Patty-Sue, and Susan. Upon arriving in Malaysia, she took up *Trish*, the name she had assumed years ago, when she first got to Amarillo.

Running away from cities and old names was nothing new to her. Wasn't that what her mother had wanted to do when Trixie became so depressed—get the whole family to run away? Get into the family car and drive nearly a thousand miles from Port Arthur to Amarillo?

Maybe it was because of her Depression. She had forgotten that. Trish put her hand on the window sill to steady herself while the memory of her depression flowed over her like a wave at McFadden Beach.

She had refused to get up in the mornings, would not eat except when her mother badgered her, and then only a few bites. She stayed in bed, her vision distorting so she became disoriented, and terrible images flooded the room. Wendy in a pool of blood—that one came often. And the bodies of Anne Theriot and James Ralston, caked over with black mud from the bottom of the Neches River. And ... and ... something else black and horrible.

Trish looked beyond the window glass at the Malaysian jungle across the river, at the monkeys leaping about in distant trees, and reached inside for the vague memory of something else. But it slipped away like a chimera, a fuzzy spot tracking on the periphery of her eye. It did no good to grope for that image, so she gave herself to what was available, of water she had once poured into a bottle and of white, a gigantic block of blank white.

She remembered vaguely how she would not go to school, talked little to her parents, would not answer the phone. And when the family doctor prescribed Valium for her, she sometimes slipped into the oblivion of dreamless sleep. She liked the Valium for the escape it offered, and she asked for more, and when her mother refused, Trixie found assorted bottles in her parents' liquor cabinet.

When the memory of tilting bottles came to her, then came the images of running tap water into bottles to hide how much she was drinking, and drinking felt good, as did sneaking more Valium from her mother's medicine cabinet. Then the sudden, frozen memory of her hands on the steering wheel of a car, a flying toward a wall.

And the white. The white that receded only when she awakened and asked for a glass of water.

"She's awake," her father said, his voice trembling with excitement. "Awake!" As is if it were some sort of miracle.

It seemed so to Trixie, also, for a darkness, troubling darkness seemed somehow lifted, replaced by her parents standing beside her bed, whispering.

She knew her parents but not the other women, the ones who said they had been taking care of her, not even her room with its several extra chairs and bare walls.

They said they were moving to Amarillo, and they had withdrawn her from school, so there was no point in her even going on campus—and none of that mattered, for she didn't remember school, didn't remember the house on Trinity Street, just off Lewis Drive in Port Arthur even when her parents talked about it as home, the one they were about to leave.

And, Trish thought, forcing her attention back to the monkeys on the distant trees, she had forgotten so much. Wendy vanished. And Lou Anne and James leaping to their deaths—even if she did not know them except from news reports—vanished. And Paul Newton. Gone, all gone into some weird black box in her mind.

But was it possible for someone to forget to much because of the car accident her parents described to her? Trish doubted it. She would ask Dr. Nik Isahak, she decided.

On her way home, she stopped in the shop houses close to the park and went into Dr. Isahak's office. After a short wait, she found herself sitting before the doctor.

"Are you ill today, Miss Trish?"

"No. But I'm not well, either. I need some answers." She explained about her memories surfacing, then told of her accident and long sleep and awakening to her family's move across Texas. It poured from her: her good friend vanishing into a snatch of memory of her bloodied form on the floor of the highschool, the loss of Paul Newton—all that had come in disjointed pieces as she stood in the classroom, alone, after Siti had told her about the troubled girls being removed from school. "Could injury in a car accident have caused me to lose so much memory, then for some of it to come back only now?"

Dr. Isahak templed his fingers. "Perhaps. But other elements might be the cause of forgetting large pieces of your past."

"What elements?"

"The alcohol and the Valium you said you took in such great quantities, maybe. Those could injure you. Or great trauma of some sort. We humans do strange things to ourselves when pain becomes too great."

"But there are still blanks. There is much I want to remember but cannot."

"Perhaps," Dr. Isahak said, "those memories will never return, that they should not return. How long were in a coma?"

"I don't know. Weeks, maybe."

"Brain injuries are often baffling," Dr. Isahak said.

That night she called her mother again. "Most of the memories have come back," she said as soon as her mother answered.

"Trish. Are you okay?"

"I think so. It was all a long time ago, mother. And it happened to a girl, not to me. Perhaps that girl needed to forget much in order to survive. But she's still inside me, that girl, even if I'm a different person, now. I think she was there all along, making me a bit crazy, encouraging me to wander from job to job when stress made me afraid."

"Trish, I have been thinking that I ought to fly over to Malaysia and be with you. There is a direct flight to Kuala Lumpur from Los Angeles—"

"No, mother. I really am doing well, considering all that has come storming out of the past in the last few days. Wendy's suicide. Our sudden move to Amarillo. But there are some missing pieces, mom, and you have to fill them in for me. What happened to Paul Newton? Did we move away and leave Paul in Port Arthur? Did he never try to find me?"

"Trish, don't look for Paul. Don't. You know enough now. Too much. Trish, I am going to catch that plane next Friday, if I can get a seat on it. MAS airlines, isn't it? I think they can put me on standby. I can fly to Los Angeles and—"

"You will do nothing of the kind, mother. If I needed you here, I would be the first to admit it."

After soothing her mother and extracting a promise from her not to come to Malaysia without talking to her again, Trish went into the living room with a glass of cool mint tea and relaxed in her favorite chair. She thought about Paul, about Wendy's warning that he was not worth a single one of her tears, about Wendy's suicide note.

There it was, she realized: the missing key. The note she had not remembered until that moment.

It was in Trixie's locker. Wendy had put it there before taking her life. Trixie had not looked in her own locker until after the funeral. She had not even gone to school for two days. When she found it, she assumed it to be an old note Wendy had left weeks before, asking her perhaps to wait at the flagpole or at the ice cream place, Nu-Zest, across the street, so they could walk home together. Seeing the note saddened her beyond words, and she nearly crumpled it up without reading it.

But she read the note, and it started a chain of events that seemed to spin wild and fast until no one could control them.

"Dear Trixie," Wendy wrote in a hurried, almost little-girl handwriting, "I will do it with my father's pistol. How is that for irony?

111

You must forgive me, for there is no way out, and I'm too tired to go on anymore. You were my only friend, my only real friend, and you deserve better than me. And you deserve better than Paul Newton. He uses girls and sets them aside and never cares about how it hurts. Too many things hurt, Trixie, too many things."

She had scrawled her name across the bottom of the page, perhaps, Trixie thought, even as she was reaching into her purse for the pistol.

Trixie went to the parking lot beyond the cafeteria, running so she could catch Paul before he left. He stood beside his red Chevy pickup. "Paul." She fought for breath, "I have to talk to you."

"Not now, you don't. I don't need to see anyone now. And neither do you."

Paul had gone to the funeral, but he sat in the back, and he refused to come near Trixie. He seemed to be working at avoiding her, and she had not had a chance to talk to him since they found Wendy beside the lockers.

"I need to talk. Please, Paul, don't turn from me. Not now."

He looked at her with cold, appraising eyes. "Okay, so we talk, but not right now. Since you seem to be all worked into a lather about something, I'll meet you at eight this evening."

"You will pick me up, then?" Trixie was disappointed, but would accept his terms.

"I didn't say that." He got into the pickup and shut the door. "I'll meet you in the public library." Paul started the engine, dropped the floor shift into first gear. "I think you know which table." He gave her a tight, small grin that Trixie thought was the coldest expression she had ever seen on anyone's face, then he drove away, leaving Trixie wounded and angry.

Trish went into the kitchen and poured another glass of mint tea. Was it all some kind of a game to him, she wondered, realizing as she had not back on that distant afternoon that Paul had staged the meeting much as he might set up a chess problem out of some book.

When Trixie arrived, she went straight to the oak table where she had first contrived to get Paul's attention away from a Russian chess book. He made her wait almost 20 minutes before he came. And then he would not let her speak, not at first.

He sat across from her and looked at her with an air of detachment. "You should not have forced me into this move, not now, not when we're grieving for Wendy."

Trixie started to speak, but he interrupted, holding up his hands in an impatient gesture to hush her.

"Hear me out. We lost whatever we had going long ago. We both know that. Before Galveston. It's over, Trixie, for you and me. We need to see other people, to date other people."

"I don't want that, Paul."

He took that news with a scowl. "Sure you do. We both do. I have already been seeing someone else, someone you knew. We were Intimate." He leaned back in his chair and crossed his arms, watching for her response. Trixie looked for a long while at her hands in her lap.

Then with slow and with measured, precise movements, she put her purse on the table, opened it, took out Wendy's note, and unfolded it. She spent some time pressing out the creases. Only then did she meet his eyes. His aloofness forced her on, though she knew it was wrong, what she was doing.

"Wendy left me a note." She pushed it across the table to him. "In my locker. I wasn't going to tell you about it, but now there isn't any reason not to." Paul kept his arms crossed and his eyes on hers. "Read it, Paul Newton. She mentions you in it. She knew you all along, better than I."

When Paul picked up the note, Trixie noticed his hand trembled, and she wanted to snatch the note away, to tell him it was all a monstrous hoax. But she didn't. She watched him read the note. He stood up, took a step back, knocking over his chair, then stood rock still, reading the note again.

Everyone in that part of the library was staring at them, but Paul didn't seem to notice. He set the note on the table and walked away, not looking at Trixie again. She watched as he went to the front of the library and vanished into the darkness beyond the door.

What did he do right then? Trish didn't know. She could remember, though, what he did later that night.

He drove to the top of Rainbow Bridge, to the spot where Lou Anne Theriot and James Ralston had chosen to leap to their deaths. He parked his pickup and got out. When a passing motorist honked at him, he got back into the pickup and drove down the bridge, pushing the pickup to its limits, according to a witness. At the bottom, he lost control, and the pickup rolled four times, bouncing along the shelled shoulder of the road beside the area where one of the oil companies had, years ago, dumped toxic chemicals in the marshy land that had been Joe Bailey's Fish Camp.

The pickup came to a rest with its wheels in the air. Gasoline dripped over the cab, and within seconds, the restored 1952 Chevrolet pickup became an orange-red torch, lighting up the highway for hundreds of feet.

The newspaper account was vivid in its detail, the reporter having interviewed a number of motorists and people who were fishing in the drainage canal beside the road. And Trixie saw the coverage on channel 10. The first image of the burning truck was shot from the top of the bridge, making the flame look like a tiny red ball floating in darkness. Then there were the close-up shots of the truck, still burning, the shadowy thing the reporter identified as what was left of the body hanging half out of a crumpled window.

It was the shadowy thing that came to Trixie in her room when her vision would blur and a disoriented feeling swept over her. Without thinking about consequences, she had tried to hurt Paul Newton for daring to break up with her, for hinting that he had loved Wendy, for looking at her with cold eyes and arms crossed on his chest. For such offenses, she had taken the note out, wanting to use her dead friend as a weapon to make Paul hurt as he had hurt her.

Back then, Trixie knew she killed Paul. First she had stood passive, allowing Wendy to fall into a despair so black that she took her own life—and Trixie knew she could have prevented it, had she been more sensitive. Then she set into motion the events that led Paul on that suicidal drive down the bridge. She knew she was responsible for the deaths of the only people beyond her parents she had ever loved.

It was knowledge she had felt she could not live with.

Trish sat in her easy chair in her house in Shah Alam and thought about the inadequate way she had gone about trying to take her own life. After the trip to the hospital and the humiliation of the stomach pump, she had reproached herself for not having the courage Wendy had, or Lou Anne Theriot and James Ralston had. And maybe even Paul had. After the failure to snuff herself out, she slipped into despondency, staying in her bed, watching her demons crowd the room.

That night, Trish slept without nightmares. The next morning, she took her books back to her classroom.

In third period, she asked Siti to see her after class.

"Yes, Miss Trish?"

"Siti, do you think it would be of any help to Nor if I visited her?"

Siti's face brightened. "Much help."

During her off period, Trish watched the monkeys in the river jungle, their dark bodies like playful shadows among the palm fronds and the fiery beauty of the tree called the Flame of the Forest. There is such peace, such passionate serenity in this country, she thought. Then why would I be in a hurry to leave?

The question seemed to be the right one to ask, and the answer that came unsought felt like a good one. Make it a challenge, Trish, she told herself: try staying in Malaysia longer than you ever stayed anywhere since leaving Amarillo, finish your contract here, then see where the next job might be.

The Bomoh's Apprentice

"I need pin," the customer said. "Something with power of the tiger and penetration of the snake. Soon I must be warlord and benefactor, bestower of a million seeds. What has old Me Sing Ng to offer?"

Chung Lee gave Mike a quick look, one Mike had learned to understand. Pay attention, Chung was saying: learn the secrets of dealing in vitality. "Pin, you say." Chung looked at the shelves of bottles behind his counter. "Very expensive." He waved at the bottles. "We have pills, many made by old Me Sing, himself. That one will put starch in the softest of silk ropes. *Biji Ketumbar*," he took down a bottle, "One of old Ng's most potent pills."

"A pill?" The customer sounded doubtful. "What does it have in it?"

"Ng is stingy with his knowledge, but he is my uncle, and he dotes on me. I have wheedled the ingredients out of him for this one." Chung pulled a slip of paper out of the bottle. "One part of goat's brain with one part each of purple rice, white peppercorns, cinnamon, nutmeg, cloves, coriander, Java long pepper, honey, and clarified butter. This is ground up with three parts of garlic, two of wheat flower and saffron and a piece of raw opium the size of a black peppercorn. These pills would get your great grandfather off of his deathbed to run fifty kilometers after anything in a skirt."

"The cost? Less than pin?"

"Less. That is correct."

"Pin is better," the customer said. "Deer's tail?"

"I have but one. From a middle-sized deer. But it would compare favorably with rhino horn."

"Not a big deer?" The customer rubbed his chin. Mike had to

116

work to keep his face a blank. He knew he would hoot with laughter as soon as the man left the store. "How long would it take to prepare? I have little time." The man looked at his watch.

"Two hours for proper preparation."

"Too long. Snake? A live snake? Perhaps one with much poison in its bile?"

"Yes, we have." Chung opened the door under the counter between him and the customer and picked up a cage containing several green whip snakes. Mike could not count them because they were lying in a lump in one corner. "The biggest does not have the deadliest bile," Chung said. "In this variety, the younger ones carry the strongest poison." Mike thought he saw, for a split second, a look of relief on the customer's face.

"The smallest, then. I must have the small one with the great power."

Chung put on a heavy glove that ran half way up his arm. It reminded Mike of the armor that police in Texas used when training attack dogs. "This one?" Chung took a snake from the cage, grasping it just behind its head. "Do you want a cup?"

The man took a step back. "It is better straight?"

"You are learned in the ways of pin, Mr. Leong."

"No cup, then."

"Four hundred ringgit," Chung warned. "Ng's pills are much cheaper."

Mr. Leong took out his wallet, pulled out some bills, and laid them on the counter. Mike picked them up, counted them and put them into the cash drawer.

"Bring that chair," Chung motioned to Mike. "Put it there. And the wooden block. There, on the counter, beside the chair, and the knife."

Mike placed the items as Chung directed, then retreated, wanting to watch but not be a part of whatever skulduggery his friend was up to.

"I must excite the snake to make his juices flow." Chung took the tail in his ungloved hand and thrust it into the snake's face until it hissed and squirmed.

Then he stood on the chair. "Approach," he commanded. Mr. Leong stepped forward. Chung put the snake's lower body on the wooden block, then with a speed that astonished Mike, he picked up the knife and sliced several inches off the tail. Blood spurted over the counter. Chung gripped the writhing end of the snake and held it up for his customer, who took the stump into his mouth.

Mike's stomach jumped, but he could not take his eyes off the spectacle. Chung held the snake's head high in the gloved hand and the lopped end in the other while the customer, blood running down his chin, swallowed his eyes closed and face impassive.

Chung put the snake's head on the block and sliced it off. He removed the glove. "You now have a hundred lighted firecrackers in your stomach. They will start going off within an hour, and the noise will keep you moving until dawn."

The customer wiped his mouth with a handkerchief and, for the first time since coming into the shop, he smiled.

When Mr. Leong left, Mike did not feel at all like laughing. "I'm not sure I could make that kind of sale, Chung."

"No problem. I will handle all the pin cases. You learn the pills and handle the cash. Mr. Fook Hing Leong isn't all that regular a customer, but he is a good one. I just made enough to shut the shop for the day, and I would do it, too—if I were a lazy Malay." Chung began chopping the snake into smaller pieces. "Unfortunately, I am cursed with the industry of the Chinese. So we stay open."

"Those look like bloody green sticks," Mike said, meaning the pieces of snake. "What do you do with them?"

"Cook them up. Sell them to a vendor who will get a fat profit selling the meat tonight to old men in Chinatown. The bile goes into medicines. It is quite poisonous." Chung pulled a tiny gland from the snake's entrails and held it up for Mike to see. "All together, there are about one hundred ringgit more to be had from *ular puchok*—this

118

snake. It is a tree snake. Malays consider it non-poisonous, but they are wrong. It has poison fangs, located at the back end of the maxilla."

Mike nodded. He was curious about what a maxilla was but afraid to ask lest Chung tell him. Chung, who held a degree in biology from the University of Houston, had the bad habit of explaining more than Mike wanted to know.

Chung's uncle, Me Sing Ng, had made a fortune selling herbs, prescribing folk medicine, and effecting cures among both the Malay and Chinese populations of Kuala Lumpur. He invested some of his wealth in educating Chung, and Chung showed his gratitude by taking over Ng's drugstore when the old man decided it was time to retire from the medical trade. Chung did, though, make a few changes in his uncle's business.

He streamlined the operation so that it became a specialty shop, catering to men who had certain delicate problems with their masculinity. It was more lucrative to handle only aphrodisiacs. "Besides," Chung had told Mike, "it is much more interesting than doling out bags of herbs, dried frogs, and ground-up fish bones to little old ladies in search for a cure for piles."

Mike remembered that statement as he watched Chung clean the whip-snake. Interesting, yes, he agreed. But so terribly gross.

Ng came down the stairs of the shop house, stopping on the last step to survey what was going on. "Pin from *ular puchok*, he observed, speaking English. "You have lighted the flames of generation, making a mere man into a dragon of virility, creating a delight for some woman. Perhaps for many women." Then, switching to Cantonese, he said, "You keep your American-who-looks Chinese longer than I would think. It would be better to turn him out, Chung. I will poison him, then give you the secret to counter the poison. That way, you save his life. You will be even, all debts paid. Then we kick him out. Politely, of course."

"English, uncle," Chung said. "Speak English or my friend Mike will think you are talking about him."

"But I am talking about the puppy." Ng saw Chung's face harden

119

and added, in English, "Of course. English is best, even for business. Chinese understand it. The smarter Malays understand it. Americans speak it, after a fashion. English is a crude, barbaric tongue, but functional in an imperfect world. A perfect world would speak only Cantonese." He shuffled into the room, dragging one foot. "What have you learned today, apprentice Michael Mendez?"

"Chung just taught me that I do not want to handle whip-snakes."

"This is true?" Ng looked at Chung. "You make the first sale of legitimate medicine all week, and your apprentice wants to go back to powdering pig's bones and rolling pills?"

"It was all the blood, Mr. Ning. I had never seen anyone drink blood like that. Right out of an animal. I don't mind selling those dead things in the refrigerator. Polar bear gonads. Skinned Arabian lizards. Seal's tails. But to hold a snake while ... " His voice trailed off.

Chung brought a chair to his uncle. Ng patted his nephew's arm, delighted that Chung sometimes showed proper respect for his elders, which in Ng's mind meant Ng himself. He sat down and scowled at Mike. "Is that what he told you that garbage is? Polar bear? And from the South Pole? The most potent ones come from the South Pole, any fool knows that. But those Chung sells? Pig testicles. From south Malaysia. Direct from the wet market in Chinatown, they are. Of course, you will swear on Buddha's tomb that they are the real thing—I'm sure Chung taught you that much. I would never sell anything but true, quality pin, but then I am retired and don't have to uphold medical standards anymore."

Mike brought a stool for Ng's bad leg. Ng grunted something unintelligible. "You are welcome, Mr. Ning," Mike said.

"Americans." Ng settled his leg on the stool. "They cannot pronounce the simplest of sounds. And do you know why? Because of the shape of their mouth. Their teeth are wrongly placed, and their tongue is hardly recognizable as human because it has been mixed with the tongue shapes and sizes of so many races. *Ng*, Mike. My name is

Ng. Say it: *Ng.*"

"Ning," Mike said.

"You hear, Chung? 'Neeng,' he says. It is the corrupt tongue and barbaric teeth."

Chung had warned Mike about Ng. "He seems to be as cantankerous an old curmudgeon as you will find in the eastern hemisphere," Chung said. "Study ways not to be offended. Learn the Chinese way of judging by deeds and paying little attention to words."

Mike wasn't sure he could believe Chung's assessment. Words, to Mike, had always been important, and he doubted he could ignore them from anyone. The first time he met Me Sing Ng, though, he decided that the old man was, above all else, a comic. Even his name was funny: Me Sing Ning. He never smiled, but that meant nothing. Many good comedians never seemed amused by their clowning. Ng certainly was funny, though Mike was not sure enough of his own analysis to laugh out loud at the old man's torrent of invective and crotchety observations.

"Mike's tongue and teeth are as Chinese as yours," Chung said.

Ng looked stricken. "Not so. He is American, a true stew-pot of genes. Anyone can look at me and see the real Chinese and at Mike and see the fake variety."

"I am going to do some business in Chinatown, uncle. Perhaps you would stay downstairs and give Mike more lessons in genetics. Mike, can you handle ordinary customers, with the help of the honorable and famous Bomoh and senseh, Me Sing Ng?"

"I think so."

"Uncle?"

"If you are asking me to come out of retirement to run your shop because you are not disciplined enough to conduct your affairs in a reasonable business-like way, the answer is no. I am an old man with a leg mangled by an idiot taxi driver and fingers twisted with age, a man who was cursed by fate to an old age of idleness. But I will sit and teach your apprentice whatever he is capable of learning."

121

Chung nodded and looked pleased. Mike smiled, but was not sure he ought to let himself laugh. There was a remote possibility that the old man was serious.

Once Chung had gone, Ng said, "You no doubt think I will not try to be guru for you. *Guru* means *teacher* in Malay, and those Malays with any sense know I am the best of medical gurus. A *Bomoh*, they called me, which is a title they normally give only to their own Malay herb doctors and medicine men. When Chung Lee was still split into a sperm and an egg, I worked as a bomoh. They trusted me, the Malays, because I do not look Chinese and so they thought I was a real bomoh, and because they believed with good reason that I was the greatest bomoh of all Kuala Lumpur. Of all Selangor."

"You say you do not look Chinese?" Mike asked, astounded.

"A wise apprentice will not interrupt the guru. I speak as bomoh now, so you are the bomoh's apprentice, until Chung returns. Then you can be again the apprentice of a seller of fake medicines. He would be *senseh*, the Chinese term for bomoh—but he loves money more than medicine. I sold genuine medicines from this shop for thirty years, and never did I sell a single fake herb or imitation anything. It was a point of honor, not to mention a matter of medical ethics. Only a dog would sell improper medicines."

"But Chung sells—"

"Yes, Chung. He is an honorable businessman. Chung knows how to make money, better than I. It is true, he puts certain substitutes into his ware. But then those who are simple enough to buy his trash deserve what they get. The fools. If a single customer were to go from this shop and use his head enough to understand he had bought fake medicines, I would shake his hand. I would insist that Chung give him his money back, three times over. But none will ever know, for they are all fools. There is no man more foolish than he who finds his rope limp. He will buy anything, eat anything to learn to make it stiff once again. And he will never question the medicine fed him. Never."

"Do you believe your medicines cure impotence?" It was a

122

question Mike had wanted to put to the old man ever since meeting him and learning the kind of operation he and Chung ran.

"Of course. Chinese have the best medicines in the world for helping men be men. Why do you think there are so many Chinese in the world?"

Mike allowed himself a chuckle, thinking old Ning was making a joke.

"You laugh," Ng said, his eyes flashing—what? Amusement? Contempt? Mike felt uneasy. "But your laughter is based in ignorance. The rest of the world laughed when they found Chinese piercing bodies with needles to cure pain. But now they send their medical men to us to study acupuncture. Using of pin—the flesh of special animals to invigorate a man lost to softness—is as old as acupuncture. And we have known of herbs and spells that work like pin for centuries before your ancestors learned to mint a coin or craft a sword."

Mike wasn't sure if Ng was teaching or clowning. But he suspected that old Ning was a true believer, whereas Chung, in answering a similar question, had taken a more sensible approach.

When Chung told Mike his uncle was a medicine man, a bomoh to the Malays and a senseh to the Chinese Malaysians, Mike wanted to know if Chung believed his uncle had any real power to cure.

"More than you might think," Chung said. "Some of the herbs he uses contain alkaloids, for example, that can reduce fever or block pain, in much the way aspirin works. And there is no way to measure how well he makes belief systems work for people. In your country, it is no different. There are medicine men who cure many ailments by making people believe themselves well."

But when Mike asked Chung about the validity of his aphrodisiacs, he had answered only with laughter.

"That man," Ng said, indicating a man approaching the shop, "Will want ground horn of the rhinoceros. One packet. He will try to cheat you on the price, but do not drop below thirty ringgits. You must handle the sale. I am retired, please remember."

"Thanks," Mike said. The advice was not necessary. Mike had watched Chung sell unicorn's horn to the man two days before. Big Wang, Chung called him. Mike thought the name a joke, but it wasn't. His name was Li Wang. And he was big. The two had bargained for almost half an hour before settling on a price for the unicorn's horn.

They called it rhino horn, but Mike knew the tradition of the magic of the unicorn. And the rhino came as close to the mythical beast as anything.

Chung told Mike after Big Wang left that the rhino horn was, in fact, the ground-up bone of a pig's leg. "Real rhinoceros horn is hard to get these days," Chung had explained. "And since Big Wang doesn't know the difference, the pig bone will light his fire just as well."

Mike located the jar with the packages of ground pig's bones just as Big Wang came into the shop. He began speaking Cantonese, but to Mike the anger in his voice was unmistakable. "Sorry," Mike interrupted. "I know only English. Please forgive my shortcoming."

"Where Chung Lee?" Big Wang demanded.

"Out on business. May I help you?"

Big Wang blustered around the shop, looking at everything with exaggerated attention. "Him come back. When?"

"Much later." Mike hoped the man would be discouraged at the prospect of having to wait.

Big Wang seemed to come to some sort of decision and calmed down. "You sell rhino horn? How much?"

Mike, relieved to see the change in mood, got the jar and took out a packet of white powder. "Thirty ringgits, same as before." Held the packet out to Big Wang.

The man took the packet and laid it on the counter. He pulled a similar packet from a pocket and emptied the contents of both on the counter top. "The same, yes?" he demanded. Mike shrugged. "The same, yes." Big Wang swept the powdered bone onto the floor, stepped back and pulled a small pistol from his back pocket. "You sell Big Wang cheap bone, not rhino horn." His voice trembled with anger. Mike figured that it was no time to argue. "Bone not work. Chuen Yuet laugh, say Big Wang not big. Say you sell trash. I have powder tested. It bone, not rhino horn. Rhino horn a wild hair, not bone. You cheat Big Wang, make Chuen Yuet laugh."

"There must be some mistake," Mike said. "I have the rhinoceros horn right here—the very one we sliced part of and ground up. Let me get it out for you." He opened the door under his side of the counter and looked at Chung's snake glove. If he put it on, Big Wang might notice he was up to something. But to grab a snake without one sounded grim. Facing that pistol was worse, he decided. He opened the cage, made a quick grab for the area behind a snake's head, and pulled one of the snakes out. "Here, I'll toss it to you." He threw the snake onto Big Wang's chest. As he let go of the viper, it got enough teeth into the back of his hand to scratch a red line from wrist to knuckle. "That snake is poisonous," he warned.

Big Wang dropped the pistol and jumped back, his face contorted by fear. He shook the snake from him as he turned to run. One foot caught in the cuff of his pants and he stumbled, his head striking the door frame with a loud crack.

The snake slithered out the door and into the sewer. Big Wang slumped to the floor, unconscious.

How did I get myself into this? Mike wondered. For a South Texas boy it seemed an unlikely career to be selling fake unicorn's horn and tossing snakes to customers on a side street in Kuala Lumpur.

He had come to Malaysia to visit his father, a petroleum geologist for ESSO. "They will love you over here, Mike," his father said. "You always complained about looking different in school back in Port Arthur. Here you'll fit right in. Most of the city is Chinese."

"But I'm an American," Mike said. His mother was Korean and his father a Mexican-American. Most people, upon seeing Mike for the first time, assumed he was oriental.

"So am I, my boy. But over here, they like my brown skin. No one calls me a spic or a pepper belly. Of course, they all expect me to speak

Cantonese."

The lure of a place where he didn't look different to everyone was too great. Mike agreed to join his father in Malaysia as soon as the spring semester at Lamar University was over.

He met Chung on his fifth day in Kuala Lumpur when Mike nearly killed him. "A Malaysian driver would have run right over me," Chung said, later. "Do you always give a motorcycle so much room when you drive?"

"Of course," Mike said. "I learned to drive in Texas, remember?"

"My luck," Chung said.

Chung had zipped past Mike on a motorcycle, going around his Toyota on the wrong side. Mike, not yet used to the wild way Malaysians drove, slowed down. Chung's bike hit a spot of grease on the road, and within a couple of seconds, he was down, skidding on the blacktop. Mike stopped, aware that traffic behind him might hit the cyclist if he changed lanes. Chung bounced to his feet as soon as he came to a stop. At that moment, he said later, he was sure that Mike's car would kill him.

Mike took him to General Hospital, where a nurse, who saw several such injuries daily, sprayed antiseptic ointment on Chung's arm and hand where the pavement had rubbed away the skin. "That's all?" Chung asked.

"Yes." The nurse spoke with a harsh edge in her voice. "Make sure you keep the wound clean. Go to a chemist for ointment. Medicine for a burn works. Don't go to a senseh medicine man like so many Chinese do." She looked at Chung, then added in a querulous, demanding tone, "Do you understand?" Without waiting for a reply, she turned to the next person in need of emergency help.

On their way out of the hospital, Chung told Mike, "If I had been bumi, she would have given me better treatment."

"Bumi?"

"Malay. But I am Chinese, so I get poor treatment from a bumi nurse at a bumi hospital."

That nurse, Mike thought, had been a little rude, though it seemed to him that Chung had received about the same treatment everyone else was getting at the emergency receiving center. The staff there was overworked. But he understood the feeling. In Port Arthur, there had been plenty of times when he was certain people mistreated him because he looked like a gook or a nip or a slope or whatever nasty term the bigots decided to hurl at him. Chung's suspicion about racism on the part of the bumi nurse made Mike feel an irrational bond with him, so he decided to cultivate a friendship, if he could.

Chung felt obliged to do something in return for Mike's not killing him on the highway. Within a week of the accident, Chung had perceived Mike's interest in his unusual drugstore and invited him to work there a while, just to learn how the trade worked.

So I come to Malaysia, Mike thought, become friends with a Chinaman I nearly killed, and the next thing I know I'm peddling aphrodisiacs and chunking a snake at a madman with a pistol.

Ng climbed to his feet, muttering and grunting. He took Mike's hand and examined it. "A man who is fool enough to grab a snake is a man who should have fangs stuck into his hand. But you have the luck of the ignorant. No puncture, and no poison. Still, your hand might rot." He pointed to a bottle on a shelf behind Mike. "Give me that medicine."

Mike hesitated as he picked up the bottle. It contained a brown goo of some sort. Did he want that on his hand? Might it be worse than the rot the old witch doctor mentioned? The scratch on his hand did seem to hurt more than a simple, ordinary Texas scratch would. His father had warned him to work at keeping any cuts clean because microbes grow at such a fierce rate in the tropics. Might the medicine man's concoction be like rubbing the wound with dirt? But then Chung seemed to believe the old man could cure some things—and Chung had a degree in biology. Mike struggled with indecision even as he handed Ng the bottle.

Ng applied some of the goo to the back of Mike's hand. A

127

pleasant, tingling warmth replaced the stinging. "I would charge you a stiff fee for my service if you were not working for Chung." Ng walked over to Big Wang and nudged him with a toe. "He sleeps like a pig in mud. If he does not awaken soon, you will drag him into the street. We cannot have customers as limp as Big Wang lying around the shop. It would be bad for business."

Irritated by Ng's refusal to comment on the clever way he had disarmed Big Wang, Mike asked, "when he is awake, will you shake his hand and give him ninety ringgits for being clever enough to spot fake medicine?"

Ng gave no sign he heard the question. He shambled to the rear of the shop, got a cloth, wet it, then went to the counter.

"That jar, apprentice Michael Mendez." Ng pointed. "Get it for me." He went to Big Wang and sat beside him on the floor. Mike brought the jar.

Ng took a handful of ground herbs from the jar, squeezed water from the cloth and worked the herbs into a rough paste. Then he washed Big Wang's face with the cloth, treating the area around the bruise on his forehead with care. Most of the paste he applied to the bruise. A small bit of it he dabbed under Big Wang's nose.

Big Wang groaned, fluttered his eyelids and said something in Cantonese.

Ng scowled. "You are to speak English, cabbage head. My apprentice does not understand your barbaric yammerings." He put a hand on the man's chest when Big Wang struggled to get up. "You don't move yet. My herbs will fall off your head, and I would take it as an insult for you to waste my medicine."

Chung came into the shop. He looked around, but asked no questions. Instead, he picked up the pistol and removed a single twenty-two shell from its firing chamber.

Big Wang grunted, then Mike saw the panic come back to his eyes. "Snake." Big Wang looked around the room. "Snake."

"You look better now. More natural." Ng wiped the poultice off

Big Wang's head. "You can get up now. Chung, this lump of pig excrement caused us to lose our best snake. Six hundred ringgits, that snake would bring. And he insulted my friend, Mike."

Big Wang stood up, clutching the door frame for support.

"Friend?" Mike whispered, amazed.

"Rhinoceros horn does not work for everyone." Chung picked up the empty packages Big Wang had swept to the floor earlier.

"Give him my *Biji Ketumbar* pills, nephew Chung," Ng said. Then, addressing Big Wang, he said, "You pay for these tomorrow, after a night of exercise with Chuen Yuet. I would give them in fair exchange for the rhinoceros horn, but you dumped it on the floor."

Chung took one of Big Wang's hands and put a packet of pills into it. He slipped the pistol into Wang's back pocket. Big Wang nodded and staggered from the store.

"I tried to teach your American apprentice some important matters." Ng hobbled back to his chair. "But who knows if anything got through his crazy-shaped American head?"

The Skulls of Chiang Mai

Cal brushed the gem seller aside and went into one of the larger stalls that had jewelry and paintings displayed for the tourists. The proprietor tried to engage him in conversation, but Cal ignored him. At the back of the store, he stopped by a glassed-in display. "Skulls, as I live and breathe. Jenny-babe, get in here and take a look at this. Silver-lined skulls."

Jenny stood out in the dirt street, eyeing with discomfort the poverty around her. The late afternoon mountain sky was iron gray, and a light mist drifted out of low clouds. A bent woman, toothless and wrinkled almost beyond belief, held her hand out to Jenny. "One baht?" she asked. Jenny produced a coin and pressed it into the woman's hand.

"Jenny, you really oughta see this." Cal kept his attention on the skulls. The display case held two of them: the top part of the skulls only, sliced off above the eye sockets. The larger one was sitting on black velvet like a turtle; the smaller, turned up like a bowl, held a few Thai coins. Both had elaborate silver work lining the edges. "Are those genuine human skulls? Where are the bottoms—the eyes and jawbones and teeth?"

"Them real," the shopkeeper said, taking out the larger skull. "Eyes, teeth no good. Throw away. Me have other skulls. Whole. No silver. Want see?" He bent to open the cabinet below the display.

"Yeah, yeah. Want see. And where the heck did you get human skulls?" Cal looked out front and saw the tour group going by. "See later. Gotta run." He went out of the shop and up the hill, after the tour group. The gem salesman Cal had pushed aside followed him.

He hoped to catch a little information from the tour guide about poppy-growing by the mountain tribe. The Thailand government claimed to have put a stop to opium production, at least this close to Chiang Mai. But Cal understood that the authorities winked at the cultivation of a plot here and there. Good for the tourist trade, he had heard.

He discovered that the villagers not only had a good source of the dope, but some smoked opium as a gimmick for the tourists, or at least a strange woman with a high forehead did. She lit up after six Americans and their guide had gone into the hut. Cal followed them, ducking to get into the doorway.

The floor was just regular earth; the walls were mismatched, ill-fit boards, unpainted and graying into jagged edges where they met the ground. The roof sagged, an eyesore of patched rust that might have once been corrugated zinc. Behind a bamboo wall sat a pile of skins and blankets. Cal pulled aside the rag that served as the bedroom door and saw a child sleeping.

"Look at that," one of the men with the group said, "she's lighting that odd pipe."

"Opium," said the tour guide. "You can try some, if you like. She wants you to take her picture so she can charge you ten baht."

"That's," the American paused to calculate, "forty cents. Fair enough." He took out his camera. Three of them began photographing the woman. Cal pulled his camera out and got off a few shots of the opium-head, then photographed the area that the guide said was the kitchen. He stepped out the door, leaving the tour group to pay for the photography session.

Outside, the gem seller held up a red stone. "Ruby," he said, "You watch." He took a piece of a mirror from a cloth sack slung from one shoulder. Cal brushed by him. He wanted to photograph a woman in highland garb who was carrying a child strapped to her back. But he did not want to pay for the privilege.

Calvin Barnlund never wanted to pay for anything. Early in life, he discovered that if he didn't save a penny when it came his way, he would later suffer the lack of power that came with being broke.

He had saved much of his salary for the years he served in the United States Army, and he managed to stay state-side, the safest way he knew of avoiding anything that might even resemble combat.

With careful investment of his savings, he started a business selling insecticides, and was successful. When his business started failing, he sold out to his partner, taking him for just over a million dollars.

Military retirement and the money he cheated out of his partner allowed to do what he always wanted: retire and travel while he was still young enough to enjoy it. Though he had plenty of money, he clung to his habits of not spending a dime unless he absolutely had to.

At age 55, Cal met and married Jenny in Singapore. The trip to Thailand was the first of what he had described to her as "a life-long honeymoon journey."

Cal waited until the tour group emerged from the hut of the opium-smoker. He figured, with accuracy, that several of them would pay the woman with the child on her back for posing.

When Cal and the Americans finished picture-taking, the woman said, "Ten baht for the baby?" The tourists produced bills, handed them to the woman. She gave them to her baby, who stuffed them somewhere into its clothing. Cal turned back toward the shop with the skulls. The woman followed, mumbling to him.

"She says," the gem seller took Cal's arm, "that you pay for taking picture."

"Those other suckers paid her well enough for us all. Tell her that."

"I tell her. Then you look at ruby?"

Cal ignored him, concentrating instead on the herd of little kids coming up the street. They crowded around him, palms up, singing, "one baht, one baht, one baht?" their voices going up with the word *baht* so that Cal thought they sounded more like chickens than children. When did not hand out coins, they headed up the hill toward the tour group, who were, in Cal's opinion, throwing their money away for permission to photograph an ugly old woman.

Jenny had watched Cal with open contempt as he chased after the American group and their guide. The shopkeeper holding the skull watched her.

A group of children, who had seen her give the coin to the old lady, surrounded Jenny, all clamoring for one baht. She placed a coin in every palm.

The shopkeeper watched the beggars and their benefactor. He slammed the skull on the countertop, turned to the wall and swung his fist with a fury that would have splintered wood and broken knuckles had he carried through with the blow. Inches from the wall, he stopped, opened his hand and patted the rough-cut board. Leaning his forehead against the wall, he took a deep breath and forced himself to smile. He turned back to the counter, leaned over the glass, and looked at his own image. The smile looked hideous. He tried again, then noted with annoyance that he had damaged the silver lining of the skull in striking it against the counter top. He closed his eyes for a moment, then with exaggerated gentleness, replaced the skull in the display case.

When he stepped into the street, he flashed Jenny a charming smile.

"You think little of him, no?" he asked, pointing up the hill where Calvin was entering a village house.

"Yes," Jenny said. She offered the shopkeeper a small, qualified smile. "I'm Jenny," she said, offering her hand.

"Call me Zul." He shook her hand. "It is short for a name that even the tribesmen here find too long to say." He looked at the sky. "It will rain before dark, and you are on a motorcycle?"

"I'm sure we'll leave soon. Cal hates to get wet. Zul, Your English is excellent, but ..."

"Missionary school. Then a hitch with the American army."

"... but you spoke pidgin to Cal a while ago. Why?"

"I was being the colorful native for the rich tourist." He grinned and held his hand up to stop her from speaking. "Why speak normally to you? Because, lady, you are not a tourist in the way your companion is."

"I guess not. Cal finds everything so ... so interesting. But he doesn't seem to see how the people he watches suffer. He is so lucky, so rich, while they," she gestured at the village, letting her voice trail off.

"Exactly so. They are poor. We are poor. My people once were farmers. Bad ones, to be sure, but they were proud, and fine warriors. They would burn a section of mountain jungle, then grow crops where the ashes gave life to the soil. When it wore out, they moved on, burning another place in the jungle. For hundreds of years they farmed and did battle with the people of the plains of Chiang Mai. My ancestors turned headhunters when they met the people of the plains—a way to show contempt for their enemies. A fierce and proud people, my tribe. But you would never know it to see them now."

"What happened to that pride? Did the tourists ruin them?"

"That, too. American soldiers came to Viet Nam and would pay much for opium. So my people became growers of poppy, and many learned to smoke opium. They became rich, for mountain people. But they forgot how to farm and lost the will to fight. Now the Thai government says we cannot grow opium, for the American government pressures them to stop us. So we sell trinkets. Many of us are beggars. Our children learn to beg early when visitors press coins upon them." Zul's eyes narrowed.

"I am embarrassed to be here." Jenny couldn't meet his eyes, and her face flushed hot.

"That is clear. I saw it in your giving the coin to my grandmother. In the look of disgust you gave to the tourist you travel with. In the handing of coins to our children. How do you come to carry so many baht coins?"

"When I moved to Asia last year, I decided that if anyone was needy enough to ask me for a coin, I would give one. I am not rich, like Cal, but neither am I so poor as the ones who want a coin. I carry many in my purse for those who ask."

Jenny thought of Cal as she spoke. She had never seen him give anything to anyone—and yet she had married him. The fact was astounding.

Calvin Barnlund had seemed so charming in Singapore, sitting across from her at Raffles, stirring his Singapore Sling, speaking with intelligence. "When you travel to a new land," he said, there in Raffles, sitting beneath the photographs of Herman Hesse, Somerset Maugham and other writers who had once frequented the hotel, "you experience life more intensely. In Peoria, I could go for weeks without adding much to my store of new experiences. Months, maybe. I think my father went years without seeing or doing anything new. But abroad, where everything is new, you're forced to look intensely at everything. Everything. Plants. Insects. Buildings. People. Especially the people. This intensity slows time down. In subjective time, you live weeks, maybe months in a single day of intense new experiences."

Yes, Jenny thought, listening to Cal put into words a phenomena she had already experienced. She looked at him with increasing respect, and the respect slipped sometime that evening into love. It didn't matter that he was 25 years older. He had wisdom, charm, and the ability to make his life longer with his understanding about the subjective nature of time.

Somewhere in the back of her mind was the knowledge that she had just lost her job teaching at Institut Teknologi Mara in Malaysia. Her department chairman had given her the news just before she went on spring break to Singapore: at the end of May, Jenny would be out of a job. But she didn't allow herself to think that her hasty marriage might have been due in part to her need for the security Cal's money would bring. She married him because she loved him. And she loved him for his wisdom, his tenderness, his intelligence.

It took only three days of traveling with Cal in Thailand to discover her mistake. He was neither wise nor tender. Intelligent? Perhaps that. Intelligent enough to travel on a shoestring when he could afford to go first-class for the rest of his life and still have a healthy estate to bequeath to heirs.

Not that she was interested in getting his money. By the time they reached the mountain village, all she wanted from him was a graceful way to part company. He had rented a motorcycle to go touring around Chiang Mai because that was the cheapest way to travel. Hire a guide? Forget it. He used Fodor's handbook as his guide when he wasn't tagging along with a group that had paid money for a guided tour.

She and Zul watched as Cal photographed the woman with a child on her back. "My wife." Zul pointed to the woman. "And my son." He sighed. "So ignorant she is. She is proud and so will not beg. But her posing for cameras degrades her, like begging."

When the children surrounded Cal, Jenny said, "He won't give a single baht."

"My father," Zul said, indicating the gem seller following Cal. "He was Head Man of the village for many years. Now he is an old man selling stones, and I am cursed with being Head Man in this time of barren fields and thorns."

Zul's father scratched a piece of mirror with a tiny stone, then snapped the mirror where he had put the scratch. Cal stopped walking. "Do that again," he said. The man cut the glass again.

"Ruby. Real stone, from Burma. I have good price. Real stone cut glass, like diamond. You have coin? I show trick."

"The trick is to get a coin out of my pocket and into yours. An old trick, one I seldom fall for."

"Use my coin, then. See, good coin. No dent. The old man knelt on one knee, put a small block of wood on the ground and placed his ruby on top of it. He set a coin on the ruby and struck the coin a sharp blow with a hammer. "Look at coin."

"I'll be damned. Jenny, you oughta look at this baht. He put one helluva dent in it. And the gem isn't even scratched."

"Real ruby. Best quality. You want? I give for only three thousand baht."

"It's pretty enough. And it for sure is harder than red glass would be. But it doesn't matter it if is a real ruby or a fake. The fact is I don't like rubies. Besides, I don't have any mirrors that need slicing up, and I've got no coins that I want to punch holes in." Cal laughed. "Not a single mirror to cut up." He laughed again. Zul's father smiled, but Jenny could see the smile was on his mouth only. His eyes glowed with resentment.

"Jenny," Cal strode up to her, ignoring Zul, "there was this funny woman in that hut who smoked opium. No kidding. Just for the tourists, so we would want to take her photograph. I guess these villagers still have a field or two of poppies around."

"You want to see poppies?" Zul asked. "Me show. You give twenty baht, me show poppies. Whole field."

"Zul, don't talk like that." Jenny's face flushed red.

"Twenty baht just to see some flowers? Too much." Cal walked into the shop to look at the skulls again. "How much for that skull, the big one?"

"Special deal for you, boss. Only two thousand baht."

"The bone is splintered and cracked. The silver work is shoddy."

Zul took out the skull and examined it. "Bone in good shape. Maybe silver loose here. I come down to fifteen hundred."

"Whatever would I do with somebody's old head case, anyway? Forget it."

Jenny turned in disgust from the haggling to look at the gem seller. "Zul told me you are his father. My name is Jenny." She offered her hand. He looked at it, not offering his own.

"You married to him?"

"Yes." Jenny felt miserable. She dropped her hand. "But don't hold it against me."

Zul's father spat on the ground. Jenny turned to watch the tour group approaching, her cheeks burning. They walked down the hill, toward their bus. Jenny thought of running after them, catching a ride wherever they were going, so long as it was away from the little village.

Cal came out of the shop. "You say how much," Zul called after him.

"See Poppy flowers grow?" the old man asked.

"Not for any twenty baht."

"Special deal for you," Zul said. "You see poppy field free."

"Free? That's more like it. But what is the catch?"

"No catch. You wife give baht to grandmother. To childs of village. We show poppy for lady."

"I don't want to see poppies," Jenny said.

"I sure as hell do. Especially if you just squandered some big bucks on these beggars."

"You will not tell me how to spend money."

"I won't give you any, either, when you throw it away being the big shot. Where are those poppies?"

Zul said something in his own language to his father, then raised his voice, calling a name Jenny was sure she could not ever hope to pronounce. Another man came from the hut across the street. "They show poppies," Zul said. "I stay. Close shop."

"Cal, let's leave. Darkness is coming, and Zul said it's going to rain."

"If you hadn't already paid for the ticket to the poppy fields, I would leave now. As it is, I'll not miss out on seeing them."

"If you go, don't expect to find me here when you come back."

Cal laughed, dry and humorless. "And just how do you plan to make it back to the hotel in Chiang Mai? Without me to get you around, sweetums, you are stuck."

Red with anger, Jenny watched the men leave. Zul shrugged and began closing his shop. "Zul, If I started now, how long would it take me to walk down the mountain?"

"You will never make it. Darkness comes. You would fall from the mountain and vanish into the jungle, forever."

"Do you have a car? Could you drive me?"

Zul moved merchandise into the store. "Why not? I take others who get stranded. For a price."

"Of course I would pay." She began looking through her purse.

"Five hundred baht."

Jenny caught her breath. She didn't have that much with her. It was only about 20 American dollars, but by local standards, it was far too much for the service Zul offered. "Three hundred?" she offered timidly, saw Zul's face harden, and added, "and twenty five?"

Zul snapped the padlock on the door of his shop. "Yes. Three-two-five baht. You wait. I get truck."

While Jenny waited, the short, tropic twilight came and went, and it started to rain. Lightning flickered here and there on the horizon, too far away for thunder. When Zul arrived in the pickup, Jenny was wet and shivering. As she climbed in, she felt her dress catch on a spring sticking through the seat cover. The material gave with a short ripping sound. "We wait. Two men come," Zul said.

Jenny looked through the rear window when she felt someone climb in the back. Two men, silhouetted against a neon flash of lightning, climbed into the roofed back of the pickup. One carried a sack that might have contained a coconut. "Isn't that your father and other the man who took Cal to the poppy fields?" she asked.

"All wild mountain men are alike in darkness." Zul started up the mountain.

His answer set Jenny's hair to prickling. "Are you going the right way? I thought Cal and I came from back there."

"I take short cut for boss lady," Zul said. He laughed a shrill laugh that frightened her. "Short cut, short cut," he said, laughing as if there was a joke she was supposed to catch. She sat in silence, growing short of breath from fear.

"Where," she asked, swallowing hard and working to keep her voice steady, "where do you get the skulls you sell in your shop?"

"Yes," Zul said, laughing again, more shrill than before, "yes."

Jenny closed her eyes and slumped in the seat. "Oh, my God," she whispered.

To Buy a Knife

As I walked through wisps of white smoke past the hawker across from Pashu-patinah Temple, I paused to look at the ceremonial daggers, and thought of Sammy.

Sammy collects knives. Or he once did, when he was still alive to me, still my son, a mere boy, poised on the edge of years of being someone else in that steaming Texas August before his tenth grade at Thomas Jefferson High School. "Try out this Malayan throwing knife," he had offered. And I did. The balance of the knife felt wrong, and when I threw it at the plywood target Sammy and I had erected behind our garage, between the fence and the canebrake, it turned only once, striking the board with its handle.

"It does that every time," Sammy had said, retrieving the knife. "It's because of the weird balance."

He had others he could stick into the center of the target at will. And still others—like the fancy one with a pearl handle, a wide, etched blade, and maroon scabbard—that were so sharp he could jam the point through a nickel.

Norman, my father, once collected knives, but not in a serious way, as Sammy had done that summer; and Norman was interested only in pocket knives. Still, I would have bought one of the daggers for the old man, if he were still alive, or for Sammy, if I could have found a way to think of him as alive.

The recollections of Norman and Sammy lasted just a few seconds while I stood in the cool Himalayan morning beside a display of merchandise meant for tourists. I shook my head when the hawker gestured toward his knives; I was no mere tourist in Katmandu, but a businessman, there to make purchases for my company, Far East Jewelry.

Then why find myself up and out so early, wandering around the city as a tourist would, and why come to this temple, the place where the dead are cremated beside the holy waters of the Bagmati River?

I walked past the hawker's stand toward the stone bridge. Maybe, I acknowledged, it was just a morbid fascination with death, or perhaps the idea of cremation, a shallow and unworthy desire to see the mechanics of the Hindu's treatment of death. Yes, that's it, I told myself, making it an accusation, an indictment.

In the center of the bridge, three boys leaned against the rock railing, elbowing each other and pointing at something below. I stepped to the edge and looked at the monkeys that had their attention, a large one and a much smaller one, copulating. One of the boys handed another a cigarette, and when I caught a whiff of the smoke, I knew they were smoking something more insidious than tobacco.

Sammy had begun experimenting with marijuana that August. He even showed me where he kept his stash in his room: a plastic bag of twig-filled leaves shot through with tiny round seeds.

"This is good shit, Dad," he said. "Want to try a couple of hits?"

I shook my head. I had smoked the stuff back in college, but then who hadn't? For me, it had been a passing interest, one to set aside when it became clear being drugged interfered with more important matters. Sammy would follow the same pattern, I reasoned.

But he did not. School began, and Sammy took to getting stoned daily during lunch, hunkering beside the Dumpsters behind the Dairy Queen with some other boys, puffing themselves into a stupor. The police caught them there, handing around a roach, and I had to go down to the Port Arthur Police Station to claim my son.

It had been the first of many similar trips, sometimes at night, once even going up the tobacco-stained cement steps of the city jail, through a couple of sliding iron doors to say a few words to Sammy, who stood with defiant and blood-shot eyes in the bull pen where police locked up petty thieves, drunks, and derelicts. Derelicts, I told myself, like Sammy, who looked out at me with a face no longer so young and innocent as he had been under the August sun when he handed me the Malayan throwing knife, not so long before.

I wanted to snatch the joint from the boys and toss it into the river below. Instead, I went to the other edge of the bridge to look at the women standing in knee-deep water, washing clothes.

Smoke from two cremations lifted a few feet into the air, then drifted back toward the temple. Was that what I had come to Pashu-patinah for? I asked myself. I walked back the direction I had come. A beggar with shriveled legs below his knees met me at the end of the bridge. He held up his hand and I pressed a coin into it, trying not to look at the man's maimed legs, trying not to let in the memories of Sammy's tale told one cold night at St. Mary's Hospital.

But, of course, it was no use; the memory flooded over me, and I stumbled from its impact, catching the wall of the temple for support. The white-washed wall I stood beside wasn't so different, in the morning sun, from the stark white walls of Sammy's hospital room when he stayed for six weeks in a live-in drug rehabilitation program for teenagers.

Parents could visit on Mondays. Sammy, sullen and angry, spoke to me not at all during my first two visits; he moved from anger to seeming indifference on the third. On the fourth, he talked, and I listened in silence there in the hospital chair beside a white-washed wall.

Grass was okay, he told me—something to stay loaded with when LSD was unavailable. But LSD was the best, for it allowed him to see interesting things. Like the way the cars in the parking lot at school all stood up and turned toward him, blinking their eyes, then became regular cars again. Like the way his hands became images of a dozen hands as they raced toward each other when he clapped. Interesting, he said. But, he added, sitting on his bed, speaking as if what he had to say was of little more significance than the fact that the Malayan knife was weighted on the wrong end, "LSD almost got me killed, once."

He had been "fried on LSD," he told me. While driving down

Ninth Avenue in Port Arthur, he saw a man shoot him the finger. "Ordinarily, I would have laughed, or maybe flipped him the bone back, and that would be the end of it," he said. But he was fried, and the gesture threw him into a rage.

He veered off the road, jumping the curb, and tried to run over the fellow who hurled the insult. The man ran down an alley, and Sammy stopped the car, grabbed a tire tool he kept under the front seat, jumped out, and gave chase.

He ran to the next street, up it toward Lewis Drive, then into another alley, where he had caught a glimpse of some movement. In the middle of the alley, he stopped to look around, and that was when he heard the popping sound and felt the sting in his leg, below the knee.

Sammy pulled up his jeans and pointed to a dark scar. "He shot me right there, and it hurt like fire."

Sammy fell, crawled to a fence at the edge of the alley, pulled himself up, and hobbled, hanging on to the fence, back toward his car. He never saw where the shot came from, nor did he give much thought right then to the possibility that more bullets could come at him. His main concern was to get home and stop the bleeding and the pain.

He remembered little of the drive home, he said, but he got there, reasoning that since it was the middle of the day, no one would be home to question him. In the bathroom he got a bottle of alcohol and an old towel, then locked himself in his room.

After taking off the bloody jeans and setting them on the towel, he took down the Malayan throwing knife—the only one left of his collection. Others he had traded for grass or LSD. He dipped the point into the alcohol, then dug out the slug.

"You just dug it out with a blade, by yourself?" I asked, astounded. Yes, he said. It wasn't so deep, for it was a twenty-two short, maybe from a pistol. He dug out the slug, then poured alcohol into the wound.

I flinched at the description, I, sitting in that sterile room beside the blank hospital wall, remembering Sammy as a child when he had

143

come to me one July fourth with a hurt hand, seeking help in dealing with the hurt. It was hard to put the two images together: little Sammy with the wounded hand, wanting help, and this older Sammy sitting on his bed, alone, digging a bullet out of his own leg with the tip of a Malayan throwing knife. I struggled with the two images while he told the tale in a kind of detached, analytical way.

"Didn't the alcohol hurt?" I demanded.

Yes. It hurt plenty, but he figured he had to do it, for there was no way he could admit to anyone the bizarre series of mistakes he had made leading up to being shot. "I had forgotten all about the incident," he said, "until I got into this program and sobered up enough to do some thinking. I could have died. That man could have shot me in the head, and I would be dead right now."

He had taken to carrying a pistol in case he ever saw the guy who shot him. Sammy had forgotten about carrying the pistol, too; he traded it for some sugar cubes and a bag of grass just a few weeks later, and he had more important things to do than remembering the twenty-two slug in his leg. Things like staying stoned and getting fried.

Remembering Sammy's tale made me dizzy as I stood by the temple wall, watching a man down the stone embankment of the Bagmati River rake a bone from a fire, pound it in a furious way, and scrape bone shards back into the flame. A little farther beyond, an old man squatted beside a body lying on top of a stack of burning logs. I wandered toward him.

Monkeys ran along the river bank in front of me, and a cow walked to another cremation area to eat flowers that had been placed there in the religious rites necessary before burning a body. I sat down close to the old man and watched the fire with him, remembering Sammy, who was dead to me.

But I tried not to think about the older Sammy whom I had abandoned. The Sammy I thought about was a little boy. He came to me one fourth of July, crying loud and wild. A dud firecracker he had picked up had exploded in his hand, bruising him, blackening the skin, and ripping the flesh in a couple of places. He danced around before me, screaming, and I soothed him, tended the wound, wrapped his hand. It was the same memory that had come to me in that hospital room when he described how he operated on his own flesh with the unbalanced Malayan throwing knife.

Sammy showed such promise while in the hospital unit for drug abusers. He was released after six weeks, and he got a job. Then he began running with the old gang—some of them the very ones he had, so long before, shared marijuana with behind the Dairy Queen. He took up staying stoned again and swallowing LSD sugar cubes and God knows what other drugs. There were ugly scenes in my home, and he left, several times, with me taking him back in, believing his lies about going straight until the night I made a clean break.

For my own sake, I told myself, I had to let go. He was no longer a boy. At age 20, he would have to take care of himself. I would live as if Sammy had died—for he had, in a way. The son I knew, the innocent and loving kid to whom I once read *Huckleberry Finn* in bedtime installments, with whom I had cut and painted a plywood target for his knives—that son was gone. He was dead, then, in a figurative way perhaps, but in my mind there was genuine finality about the loss. There had to be.

I moved to Houston to avoid seeing him, and saw to it that Sammy had no address or phone number with which he could contact me when he was in the need of conning me again for drug money. I had run out of energy, out of the will to give to that drug-abusing man who by some base alchemy had grown from a boy once my son. I cannot, I affirmed again and again, find any way to approve of any part of Sammy's life.

Sammy had found, somehow, my office phone number, and had reported to me through my secretary several more ups and downs in his continuing saga with drugs. I listened to the secretary's reports only because of her insistence, but I refused to speak to Sammy on the phone or to write to him. The refusal sat sour in my stomach each time.

It puzzled me that he bothered to keep me informed about anything in his life when I had been so clear in my disapproval. The last word I got was when I phoned the home office from Tokyo, just before flying to Katmandu. He had called the secretary again, this time not bothering to ask if I would speak with him. "Tell Dad," he said, "that I have given up drugs. Not forever. Just for one day at a time." He claimed to have found a job and to have a new set of friends, ones who did not take drugs and who were bent upon helping him stay clean. "I always thought it would be easy to give up grass," he told my secretary, "but grass was the hardest. I've been sober for two months and three days."

I didn't even ask if I could believe the report, for Sammy was dead. And you don't have to deal with dead people, I told myself, feeling the sour forming in my stomach.

The man squatting beside the funeral pyre glanced at me, nodded a greeting, and seemed as if he would say something. I gestured toward the fire. "Your father?" I asked, wanting to help him allow himself permission to speak. I knew that in the ritual of cremation, the oldest son was the one who lit the fire and tended to the burning of the body.

Norman, my father, had died just months before, and I had mourned his passing, as a son must. But he had been old and tired and often in pain. It was time for Norman to die, and I had mourned in the ceremonies surrounding death not for his having died but for the loss of the relationship I once had with a man who had not existed for years. Perhaps, I told myself, this Hindu man, who seemed older than I, was laying to rest an old father, just as I had done, but with more dignity than American funeral practices allowed. Such stoking of fires and burning of bodies seemed more civilized, healthier to me than the way the funeral home in Port Arthur had tried to mask death, to deny it with the preserving of the body in chemicals and in a coffin that would stave off proper decomposition for hundreds of years.

The man picked up some straw and laid it over one foot that

protruded from the fire, then returned to squat beside me. White smoke drifted toward us and down river, in the direction of the current. "Your father," the man asked, "did he die?"

"Yes."

"And you tended his funeral pyre. That is why you asked. It is a sad business, to watch the body of your own father turn into smoke and ashes."

"We do not do it so in my country. I watched my father lowered into a grave. Burning would have been better."

"Yes. Better for the dead. The spirit comes to so love the flesh that he will linger with the body. We must utterly destroy the body to free the spirit." We sat in silence for some time, both watching the flames. "I understand loving the flesh," he said, his voice breaking.

"Yes," I said.

"You, do you have family left? A son to tend your fire when you are old?"

The question startled me. I considered it then shook my head, realizing even as I did that his attention was on the fire and he did not see the gesture.

He is dead, and that's the honest-to-God truth, I told myself. Maybe Sammy had never before claimed to have stayed clear of drugs for any length of time—except for the short stint in the drug-abuse program, of course, but how could I believe him? How could I set aside all the past betrayals long enough to consider if he were for a fact reforming himself? Better, far better to think of him as dead. A familiar sour feeling formed in my stomach.

The man looked at me after a long silence. "No son, then. Dead?"

"Yes." I told myself it was the easiest way, though at that moment disapproval of Sammy didn't feel so easy.

"I understand the pain." He pointed at the funeral pyre. "What remains of my son's body is even now turning into ashes." His voice broke, and he wiped his cheek, leaving a black smudge. He stood up and added logs to the fire.

I watched, trying without success to imagine myself feeding the fire with Sammy lying there in the flames. The man returned to my side, but we found nothing else to say. I sat on the stone embankment for perhaps an hour while the withered man stoked and rearranged the fire, adding fuel, and smearing black ashes on his cheeks from blackened hands.

Then with great effort, I stood and walked back toward the bridge. My clothes smelled of smoke, and a light layer of white ash had settled on my arms and hands, feeling wet and slippery as if I had bathed in the ashes of the dead.

At the hawker's stand I examined the knives. One in particular caught my attention, a rudely-made piece with a blade ground from a hacksaw and a handle cut from bone that was charred and nicked in spots. It wasn't the prettiest knife there, but it had been crafted by hand and had an elegance about it. When I hefted it, the balance was perfect. Its scabbard, flashy from a distance, was the work of a beginner, the tin shaped and fashioned in a crude way around a piece of rawhide. But to my mind the knife was superior to the others on display, superior to the slick, machine-stamped blades with plastic handles and rhinestones. It was without doubt, I realized, superior to the ill-balanced Malayan throwing knife Sammy and I had once struggled to throw at the plywood target in our back yard; and at that moment I knew why I had come to Pashu-patinah Temple, the place of the dead where white smoke brushed the waters of the holy Bagmati River.

I bought the hand-made knife, paying the first price the hawker named, much to his surprise. But I wanted that knife, and wanted it right then, regardless of cost. Walking away from Pashu-patinah Temple, I examined with approval the unpolished blade, the nicked handle, and the hand-crafted scabbard.

A Magic Pig

When I woke up, the King of Monkeys was sitting on my chest. It held a hand close to my nose and grunted. The King must have weighed thirty pounds, and judging from the ache in my midsection, he had been sitting there for some time.

Where was Joko in such a moment of need? I glanced around and located his sprawled form, his head propped at a terrible angle on the root of a tree.

My mind was foggy and my chest hurt from the King of Monkeys using it as a perch. For a few seconds there, I thought that Joko might have been right, after all: the island was a nightmare of black magic, and I was caught in the worst kinds of spells. "Get off of me, you furry ape," I rasped. The command was supposed to come out as a threat, but my vocal chords weren't functional, and I was shocked to hear myself grunting like an animal.

"Huh, huh, huh?" The King of Monkeys asked, thrusting its hand under my nose again. I willed my arm to shove him off, but not much came of it. The control wasn't there.

"That a magic monkey?" Joko asked.

"Not this time. Just the regular Monkey Forest variety, I think. Can you get up and knock the ugly toad off of me? My arms are asleep or something."

"No can, Boss. You wait. Arms wake up. Legs. Then we fix king monkey. Have tasks?"

I strained to make sense of his question, at the same time trying to roll over some to get the monkey to move. A pebble under my back seemed to be turning into a knife, and there were lumpy things under one hip. "Tasks? You mean tusks? No, Joko. This one seems to be flesh and blood. Not like the others. Get off, you bloody gorilla. Go mug a tourist."

"Huh, huh, huh, huh," it said. Again the hand came toward my face. It showed a staggering abundance of teeth and hissed: "Heeeeeee."

"Monkey say want peanut," Joko translated. "You no give peanut? Bite."

"Joko, must you always be a bearer of good cheer?" I tried the arms again, this time managing to get them off the ground several inches. The Monkey King took exception to my efforts and jumped on me a few times, knocking the wind out of me. "When I recover from the *dukum's* spell," I gasped, "I'll impale you on a water buffalo's horns."

"Close eyes," Joko said. "King Monkey see sleep. Wait. Arms, legs forget magic. Get stick, there, you small stick, me big. Jump Boss monkey, club head whack whack."

I located the sticks Joko referred to, lying on the ground between us. Not a bad plan, I thought, closing my eyes and relaxing as well as possible for a man with a thirty-pound monkey on his chest. The King jumped a couple more times, then settled down to wait, just as Joko said it would.

The amazing thing wasn't that I was lying there in Bali's Monkey Forest, paralyzed, with an extortionist monkey on my chest—but the fact that I was entertaining the idea that Joko had been right about the black magic.

I had met Joko on a *bemo*, a clap-trap of a van that Balinese use in lieu of a bus. He tried to get a conversation going, flashing his charming smile and getting out a few words of pidgin English. When he got stuck for a word, he would pull an Indonesian-English dictionary from a pocket and flip through it. I nodded and smiled, but paid little attention to his efforts, concentrating instead on watching nude Balinese bathing in the sewer ditch they called a river. When the river took a turn toward a rice field, away from the highway, I focused on what he was saying, trying to remember enough to make some intelligent remarks.

Not that it was much use. Joko spoke in short bursts of

monosyllabic words, getting the accent on the few longer ones he tried in the wrong place. He helped out his communication by waving his hands, raising his brows, and grinning. I understood almost nothing of what he labored to say. Nevertheless, before getting off the bemo, I had agreed to eat at Lucky's, the restaurant where Joko's mother cooked.

I got to Lucky's that evening. Joko joined me as soon I came in, sitting at the table and pouring out his torrent of broken English: "Me ver' glad you," he thrust his finger at me, "come. Food good me told madda," another finger thrust, "you come. Eat. Friends come. Me many friends. Here." Grin, grin.

Joko was taller than most Indonesians; at nearly six feet, he more resembled the Australians in height than his fellow islanders. But the similarity to the Aussies ended there. Joko was dark as an old penny, a healthy, attractive dark that some few anglos are able to cultivate by lying in the sun for years. His hair was black as stained teak, except in the sun, where it glowed an impossible shade of purple. His face looked like the Balinese fisherman that the local wood carvers liked to sculpt for tourists: high cheek bones, a thin, perfectly-formed nose, and slight creases in his cheeks that dimpled when he smiled. Which was often. Around one ear he wore a series of silver rings, a couple of which clamped over the top of the ear like shields. The total effect was of a good-looking youth, almost a caricature of the beautiful south sea island male.

We visited, if you can call it that, over a meal of rice and shrimp. But it wasn't until I hired him as a guide that he warmed to the subject of black magic on the island.

We toured on motorcycles, stopping whenever I wanted to take some photographs. During most photography sessions, Joko practiced his English on me.

"No climb banyon tree," Joko warned, taking my arm when I started to go up the tree.

"Huh?" I said, startled that he would presume to grab my arm. I glared at his hand, but he did not remove it. "That," I pointed to a spot above a primitive altar carved by some superstitious Balinese on the side of the tree, "would be a great place for a photograph of the rice terraces."

"No climb. Tree magic. Tree spirit catch toe, pull foot. Fall. Break head. Die."

"Nonsense. I want that angle for my camera."

"Pig come, eat body. Magic pig. Joko friend—finished. No climb banyon tree." He tightened his grip on my arm and pulled me away from the tree, like a life guard saving a drowning man.

We continued the conversation over lunch in a tourist restaurant in Ubud. I ordered jaffles for the two of us. The fact is, I had no idea what a jaffle was, which is why I ordered them. Some native main course, judging from the price and the position on the menu. I wanted to experience as much as possible the kind of life these Balinese led, including eating their food.

"If the spirit of the tree killed me," I asked, "why would a pig eat my body?"

"Not pig. Magic pig." He seemed to think that explanation enough.

"But why eat my body?"

"Turn dead tourist to live pig. It bad for magic pig eat body. You spirit stuck in pig, become pig. Maybe for hundred years. Thousand." Joko glanced around.

I tried to lighten up the conversation with some humor. "What would be so bad about being a magic pig?"

Joko looked at me, startled and not at all amused. "Ver' bad. Pig hurt people. Not care. If magic pig come in house and see money," Joko put his finger to his eye, then pointed at the table, boxing his fingers around a stack of imaginary money; the gesture was so eloquent that I could almost see the stack of rupia notes, "money finished." He turned his palms up, shrugged, and pretended to look around for the vanished money. "Magic pig steal. That bad."

Our waiter seemed to be staring at us, but I paid him little mind.

Probably he was just curious that a tourist was dining with a local boy. Joko noticed the waiter's attentions, too; he kept glancing at the fellow and seemed to be a little tense.

Our jaffles turned out to be some sort of sandwich. Instead of bread, the sandwich was wrapped in a crisp pancake. Inside were some unidentifiable meat, brown sauce, and sliced mushrooms. It was delicious, so I decided not to risk ruining the meal by finding out what kind of meat was in the jaffle.

"You really believe all this hocus-pocus black magic stuff?"

"Balinese not believe. Know."

"What other magic is there around?

"Much. Man see woman. Want marry. Her no see him. Him go to *dukum*, her make magic. Middle of night. Cemetery. Her dress white, call spirits. Woman notice man. Might marry."

"The witch arranges the marriage by casting a love-spell on the woman?"

"No. Only make her see man. Then up to him. But not good, sometime. Sometime child born ..." he flipped through his dictionary. "Deaf armed."

"Does a marriage from a love-spell always result in the couple having deformed children?"

"Don't know. Sometimes can't tell. No. Not always."

Joko seemed to be taking all this magic crap a bit too seriously. A good dose of doubt from someone like me might plant the seeds of intellectual growth in him. I found myself questioning his intelligence. What little he was born with seemed crippled by primitive superstitions. Still, he might be bright enough to think I was somehow trying to steal away his beliefs if I became too obvious in challenging his superstitions. Maybe clowning with him would be the right approach to expressing doubt.

"Joko, I happen to know for a fact that your parents got married as a result of a love-spell. And you are as flawless a physical specimen as the island could produce."

"How you know? Bout magic marriage?" He was startled.

"A joke," I said. "I really don't know anything. I made a joke about your parents."

He laughed, relieved. "You right, Boss. Me fadda see *dukum*. *Dukum* make magic. Midnight, in cemetery. Then me madda see him. Marry. How you know me not deaf armed, not..." he looked through the dictionary. "Cursed." He scowled at the page, flipped more pages. "Cursed to seeing." His frown deepened; he shrugged and grinned.

I was startled at the turn my attempt at humor took and for a few seconds was tempted to see more in his words than could be there. But no, I told myself: Joko is a simple, uneducated islander. What he just said had to be a quirk of using the language dictionary, nothing more.

On the way out of the restaurant, we saw a bent-looking Balinese man standing under a banyon tree near our motorcycles. He wore white from head to foot, except for a single, enormous black eye patch. The fellow was so striking that I wanted a picture of him. As I took the camera out of the bag strapped to my belt, the man lifted the patch and looked at us from two good eyes.

Joko leaped on his cycle, kicked it into life, and roared off shouting, "Follow me, Boss." I fired a couple of quick shots at the man with the patch and hastened after Joko.

He rode the cycle harder than I was comfortable with on the narrow roads, but I kept up through several turns, past some dense jungle, by an assortment of rice fields, into an area darkened from high trees. I caught up with him where the road turned into a path.

"Monkey Forest." Joko assumed the role of guide again. "Buy peanuts? Monkey know tourist. Want peanut. Steal purse. Earring. Give peanut? Monkey give purse. Earring."

A vendor with a carved wooden chess set appeared from a hut, followed by a Balinese girl with a tray of peanuts in plastic bags. The chess vendor I ignored. From the girl, I bought a small bag of peanuts.

We walked the jungle path. "What was that business about the man with the eye patch?" I asked. "Are you scared of the evil eye?"

"Him not man. Him pig. Maybe monkey." I assumed the man to be someone Joko knew and did not like—an old rival from elementary school, perhaps. Or I assumed that until Joko added, "Him magic pig. Monkey. Don't know."

Monkey Forest turned out to be a place where the island's monkeys found it easier to make a living from tourists than from whatever monkeys do for a living. We came upon a dozen or so taking handouts from a couple of tourists. An Australian woman offered a peanut to the biggest monkey. "Him King of Monkeys." Joko nudged me, holding me back. "That monkey boss. Watch."

The King of Monkeys, the dominate male of the tribe, pretended to reach for the proffered peanut, made a sudden lunge, and grabbed the plastic bag in her other hand. They had a brief tug-of-war. The King of Monkeys bared its teeth, hissing and grunting. "Let have, let have," Joko warned. "Monkey bite leg."

The other monkeys took to howling and fussing. One in a tree above us broke a branch and hurled it at the woman. It hit Joko. The woman retreated.

The dramatic episode left me dizzy. I would feed the monkeys later, I decided, stuffing the bag of peanuts into my hip pocket. As we wandered on down the jungle path, I began stumbling. "Joko," I said, "I feel really strange. All the business with the monkeys threatening the woman, I guess. Let's find a place to rest."

"Me strange, too. Sit there," he pointed at a giant root that ran along the ground several feet from its tree.

By the time I sat down, the world was tilting at a disconcerting angle, like I was coming down with an inner ear infection. "Joko, I must be getting sick."

"Not sick. Magic. Me look." He vanished into the dark jungle. Trees leaned, brushing their tops to the ground, and the sky shifted to purple and green. When Joko reappeared, the trees righted themselves, and the sky disappeared. Sunlight drifted down in wet golden globes, each hitting the jungle floor with a loud smack. Drops of light splattered on my clothes.

"Magic pig come. You hide money." Joko stumbled, falling beside me. "Maybe magic monkey. Give camera." He took my camera and slithered like a snake behind a tree, returning in seconds. "Now money. Too late, Boss. Magic pig." He pointed. "Money finished."

A man with a pig's head came up the path. As I watched, his feet became hooves. The pig man wore white clothes and had pink fur, except for a large black spot over one eye. Behind him came a regular man, one who looked familiar. "Him magic monkey," Joko said. The man's face distorted, falling out of shape like a blob of jelly. The features reassembled themselves into those of the King of Monkeys. "Monkey have tusks," Joko said. And, even as I looked, it grew enormous ivory tusks, two hanging down to its chest, two curling up past its eyebrows.

"Dancing," Joko said: "dancing." His voice sounded insane. But then the nightmare for which he was color commentator was insane. Pig and Monkey began to dance around me. The jungle joined their dance, and sunlight flashed disco colors, setting the swaying leaves aglow like lint under black lights. Pig put a hoof on my chest and shoved. I fell in slow motion into a lake of warm jelly, floated, slept a dark and dreamless sleep.

And awoke with the King of Monkeys sitting on my chest.

I ran a check on various muscles without opening my eyes lest the beast on my chest start jumping again. Or threatening to bite me again. Everything seemed functional. The rock under my back gouged worse than ever, and the lump under my hip seemed to have gotten bigger.

Then I remembered. That lump was a bag of peanuts. I opened my eyes. "Huh, huh, huh?" The King of Monkeys asked, again holding a hand under my nose. I focused my eyes with effort on the hand. It held a silver ring with a moonstone setting.

"Magic gone, Boss?" Joko asked.

"I think so."

"Get stick. Jump Monkey King. Knock head whack whack?"

"No. He's offering me a logical business deal. Wait." I edged over enough to pull the sack of peanuts from my hip pocket.

"Huh, huh, huh." The King of Monkeys watched my hand. I pulled out the bag. It snatched the peanuts from me, slapped the ring on my forehead, and leaped to a tree. The kick from its jump left me gasping for breath.

"Monkey give ring," Joko said.

"Yeah. My own. It must have taken it off my finger while I was out."

"Now you broke. Magic pig see money."

I felt for my wallet, knowing even as I reached that it was gone. "My camera, too?"

"Magic pig no like. Magic monkey like."

I sighed. "So I lost the camera."

"No lost. Got." He retrieved the camera from some underbrush behind a tree. "Sorry for money."

"Joko, you are a prince. I would rather have the camera than the wallet. All it had in it was around four hundred bucks."

Joko whistled. "That over six hundred fifty thousand rupia. You rich like," he pulled the dictionary from a pocket, flipped through it. "Emperor. Like emperor." He grinned.

Though I was grateful for his saving the camera, I looked at him with some contempt. If he would just work to cure his ignorance and get over his superstitions, he could find a way to earn more money. I almost felt embarrassed about his being so impressed by four hundred lousy bucks. Joko wouldn't make that in six months.

But I conferred greater respect on his intellectual abilities for doing the tricky currency conversion in his head.

Stiff and sore, we made our way back to the motorcycles then over the jungle road through Ubud, Denpasar, and on to Kuta, where my hotel was. I spent the trip pondering the experience in the forest. Magic was out of the question: Joko might turn to the occult for an explanation of everything from love to in-grown toenails. But I am a product of the twentieth century, of the rational spirit, of the principle of scientific inquiry. Logic ruled my life, and I had faith that there was a logical explanation to the coming of the so-called magic pig and monkey, no matter how convincing an irrational explanation might sound.

The next day, Joko rang my room early. "Rent cycle?" he asked. "Go to volcano? To Tanah Lot temple? See holy snake?"

No, I said: I had enough of unusual animals for a while.

"Have lunch. Talk. What time?"

We agreed to meet at noon in Lucky's. I had to decide about filing a report with the police, but was not quite sure what to tell them. What could I say? That a magic pig and a tusked monkey-man waltzed around me in an enchanted forest?

After taking my film to a quick-print shop, I spent the morning dodging hawkers on the beach and body-surfing the breakers, coming to no decision about a police report, though I did work out what happened to me at Monkey Forest.

At noon, I met Joko in Lucky's.

"How you like Balinese magic?" He asked. "Now?"

The question irritated me. "You looked for no logical explanation, did you? Magic explains everything that mystifies you. In a hard world, you make life worse by having to deal with invisible powers. You could simplify your life by seeing things as they are. There is no magic, Joko. No magic. What happened to us was a result of drugs. That waiter in Ubud? He slipped some nasty little mushrooms into our jaffles. It was he who came up the jungle path to rob us—I recognized him before your suggestions made my drugged mind see him as a monkey. And the pig. Not a pig at all. A man—the same one who tried to hoodoo you with the eye patch. I have a photo of him. Here." I pull the photo from my pocket and thumped it on the table in front of him. "Take a good look. He is just a man, no more a magic pig than I am. There is no magic."

I became aware that I was almost shouting, that people in the restaurant turned to stare. I lowered my voice: "Joko, do you understand even a word of what I am saying?"

For once, Joko sat somber, unsmiling. He pushed the photo away from him. "Joko understand. You," he jabbed at me with his index finger, "no understand nothing. Angry. Think Joko fool cause him no talk English. Him," Joko leafed through his dictionary. "Simple. Joko not simple. You simple. Joko know pig. Monkey. You think man rob? Man not rob. Drug? Man not drug. Monkey drug. Pig steal. Man use magic mushroom drug? Steal? Become not," he located a word in the dictionary, "human. Become monkey, pig. No human no more."

The speech astounded me. "Then you don't believe in magic, after all? You use the language of magic as a figure of speech to explain the unexplainable." It was my turn to whistle. "Very sophisticated. But why do that? Why talk so much about magic when you know there isn't any such thing?"

His face flashed anger and contempt. "You no understand nothing Joko say." He stood up. "Joko born to magic marriage. Deaf armed. Cursed to know. You born, born," he jerked his dictionary up, found a word, "blind. You born blind."

He clinched his fists and walked out into the fierce Bali sunshine.

Ceremonial Stones of Fire

"This earring once decorated the ear of a pirate from Malacca," the Chinaman said. Allen smiled but said nothing. He had dealt with this huckster, Yim Choy, before, buying British trade dollars, Thai baht, and other old coins from him, and always the man had some outrageous story about the origin of what he sold. Allen often valued the stories more than the man's merchandise. "This piece," Yim Choy held up one of the opal earrings. "He wore it like this." He held the ring against his ear and grinned.

"Perhaps," said the old man beside him. "Perhaps not." Yim Choy scowled and waved his hand, but the man went on: "There is no way to know which of the earrings the pirate wore. And it is not an honorable thing for the jewelry that such a man once had it on his accursed body."

"Antique jewelry, sir," the huckster assured Allen. "And fine gold. Pure, pure. Twenty-four carat."

"No," the other man said. "Not pure gold." Allen turned to the older man, curious that he would disparage his friend's merchandise.

"Maybe not pure, then. Twenty-two carat." When the old man shook his head, Yim Choy added quickly, "Or perhaps eighteen. Good gold. Good."

Again the old man shook his head. Allen inspected him and found himself looking into the dark, intelligent eyes of a man who seemed to have a kind of profound sadness about him.

"Many call me Weng," he said, offering his hand across the café table.

"Allen Harrison." Allen took the hand, finding it leathery and tough, a hand accustomed to work. "I would like to hear more about the history of the jewelry." He looked again at Yim Choy.

Allen came often into the Sun Wah Café in the Chinatown section of Kuala Lumpur. He bought silver coins minted in the nineteenth century, and he often purchased gemstones. The stones came from Nepalese Grukah tribesman who somehow managed to get raw stones from Burmese smugglers in Thailand, haul them to Jaipur to be cut, then take them to Kuala Lumpur to sell to tourists along Petaling Street. More important, though, Allen came to the Sun Wah to hear tales he could work into the short stories he wrote about life in southeast Asia.

That day, he had sat at one of the tables in the Sun Wah, hoping to find among the Grukahs one who had some gemstones of good enough quality to have set in gold as a gift for his wife, Ana, for their upcoming wedding anniversary. Burmese star sapphires, perhaps. Or a spinel ruby of high quality. But he found nothing suitable, and after about thirty minutes of looking at inferior stones, he felt ready to give up. At that moment, the huckster had touched his shoulder and placed a set of opal jewelry on the table in front of him.

He saw the stones in the earrings and ring flare with color, even in the dim light, and all burned with brilliant opal fire when he held them to the light. Excellent stones, he knew, all of them. He found the jewelry perfect for his needs, so he frowned, pushed them aside, and said, "I don't know about those." Allen had learned from experience that if he appeared taken with an item in the Sun Wah, he would end up paying twice or three times what he might pay if he had to be convinced to buy.

The Grukah who had been showing Allen some low-grade star rubies, moved aside, perceiving that Allen and Yim Choy had begun the ceremony of negotiations for a sale. Yim Choy had sat down, motioning to an old man to join him at the table.

"I don't know the whole story, but Weng," Yim Choy nodded toward the old man, "might know. He brought the stones from Malacca and hired me as broker for them. Look. Good stones. Good gold— eighteen carat."

"Not eighteen carats," Weng said. "Fourteen for the ring and necklace stone. Ten carats for the earrings. And not antique. Old, perhaps, for I knew the man who had them made, and I am no longer so young. In Malacca, people called him Tuck. A young man with dreams. A man who loved a woman not chosen for him by his parents. A man who was little more than a boy, and yet he dealt with pirates." He fell silent. Yim Choy started to speak, but the old man leaned forward and silenced him with a slight gesture of his hand. Allen sensed an unusual story here, and felt the hair on his neck prickle as Weng began talking.

Here was a man who knew the drama in his story, and spoke with the eloquence of a born story teller. He told of Din Othar and Tuck, sailing a junk at twilight in the Straits of Malacca far from sight of land.

Din spoke a single word: "Pirates." Tuck heard the tension in his voice, yet still did not believe Din could be serious until he pulled hard to the right, bringing the junk around. As Tuck started to stand, Din snapped, "Down. Stay down. Perhaps we can save your life. They come too swiftly for us to run. Wait until I tell you, then slip over the side. Hold to the rudder and do not make noise, no matter what you hear. Darkness comes, so you have a fine chance of not being seen at all, even if one of those scoundrels looks over the side."

"What of you?"

"This pirate has robbed me before when he caught me alone. He has no love of killing a man as old as I, even if he is Chinese and I a Malay. But you, ah. You he would open up your lungs with a *kris* just to hear them whistle away the wind of your life. Mr. Tan Hock Sin respects little, least of all those who possess youth."

The name *Tan Hock Sin* gave Tuck a chill. In Malacca, it was whispered about that Hock Sin stole from fishermen and merchants at sea, but few people believed it. Hock Sin made money from a legitimate business with buying and selling carpet. Yet Tuck's father had believed the stories, and had even claimed that Hock had something to do with the Japanese knowing about the money Tuck's family had hidden in the bamboo under their house. In Tuck's mind, Hock Sin had been the cause of his family becoming so impoverished, a condition that led to the death of Tuck's father.

"I knew Hock Sin's parents," Din said. "His mother—so beautiful, but she had a sharp tongue. On the night of her wedding with Hock Sin's father, one of the candles beside the marriage bed went out, so everyone knew their marriage would be cursed with strife. Her husband beat her, and she flayed him with her tongue. Loud were their quarrels, and long. Hock Sin grew up in a house of noisy and ugly fighting. It is no wonder he became a pirate."

Tuck began crawling toward the bow of the junk where he had hidden a fortune of a special kind in the bottom of an iron box. In that box, wrapped in a silk cloth and snapped inside a red silk purse was the jewelry that would allow Tuck to marry with dignity and pride. "Better not go up," Din warned. "Hock Sin and his men will see you. Likely they will begin shooting, even from where they are. They carry M-1 rifles."

That jewelry had come hard for Tuck, who had smuggled goods from Sumatra into Malaya, sailing in a junk hardly large enough for the open waters of the Straits of Malacca. The work had more than its share of risks, especially with him sailing alone, and always returning to Malaya at night to elude the police. He risked sudden storms as well as the police, and some of the other smugglers warned of pirates. But such threats seemed abstract to Tuck, who would take any reasonable risk to get the money he needed to get married.

The young woman he pledged himself to knew of his obsession with buying jewelry as a gift for the tea ceremony and the wedding, and she hinted that jewelry was not so important. But she was wrong about the matter. Tuck forgave her for that, for she was not Chinese, so she could not possibly know the importance of the gift.

She lived out at the old Portuguese settlement, south of Malacca, among people with weird names and odd customs. Tuck had some trouble saying her name. "Gunsalas Aeenda," he had said when they first met and she told him her name. She laughed. Her first language was Portuguese, his was Hokkien. Both spoke Malay and English, and both preferred to converse in English.

"Anita Gonzales," she corrected. "The family name goes last."

"A barbaric custom," Tuck's mother told him later. "Everyone knows the family name should go first so it can get more honor. You will teach this Aeenda to say 'Gunsalas' first, la."

"When we marry, she will take my name." Tuck smiled as his mother tried to digest that information. She asked him about it for days, finding it hard to believe that a woman would give up something so personal as her own name, even for the sake of marriage. "It is the custom of the Portuguese," Tuck said, "and she wishes to follow that custom, just as I wish to follow many of the customs of our people when we marry."

The most difficult thing for his mother had been accepting that he would choose his own wife. Young people were doing that more and more, but the fact that others did something so foolish did not mean her son should, also. She had tried to arrange a proper wife for her son on three occasions, but the negotiations broke down when the other parents discovered what had happened to Tuck's branch of the Chee clan.

Chee Soon Fah had been forced to trade his Malay currency for Japanese script. Trade your money or be killed, the soldiers told him. They followed him to the length of bamboo under his house where he kept the main cache of his money. The amount was so large that they were quite satisfied that it was all Soon Fah had. A much lesser cache lay in a tin under the earth just feet away—the money Tuck later used to buy his smuggler's junk. Within months, the Japanese were kicked out of Malaya, and Soon Fah found himself holding worthless paper. His carpet business was gone, the shop having been looted. He died soon after, bitter and poor.

When Tuck began seeing Anita, his mother objected, then gave up, feeling defeated by her own failure to get him a wife and by her inability to control Tuck since his father died. She thought it best to smile at the barbarian woman, and to offer Tuck her own wedding ring since he could ill afford gold.

Tuck looked at the metal box just two meters away and weighed the risk. What good would the opals and gold do if he were dead? And there was a chance the pirates would not find them. Not much of a chance, he admitted—but something of one. "Now," Din said. "You must slice into the water, now quietly, like a knife."

As he went over the side of the boat, Tuck heard rifle fire and men shouting. He went under the curve of the stern, as Din had directed, and grasped the rudder. When Hock Sen and his thieves climbed aboard with Din, Tuck could hear every word they spoke.

"Old man," Hock Sen said, "again the stars put you in my waters. What might I take from the philosopher of Labuhanbilik this time?"

"I have nothing of interest. You may have the boat, if you wish to be cursed with a fat, barnacle-encrusted rock that hangs between sinking and floating, even when empty of cargo."

"Poh Chu, look below. Ah Chai, search the deck. Old man, you do ride too high. What do you carry?"

"Air. That fool of an owner pays me to sail his junk from Medan to Malacca with nothing aboard. Rich men are all idiots."

"No one goes across the straits empty. Poh Chu."

"Nothing below except bilge water and rats."

"Ah Chai?"

"Nothing. Only a locked metal box."

"Break it open. Old man, I must relieve you of your pay."

"I have but a few coppers. You may have them with my blessings. If you want the silver that fool promised me for delivering his boat, you must come to my home in Labuhanbilik when the moon is full."

"Gold. In the bottom of the box. Gold and stones that give light. But so little gold. Not enough for a week with a whore in Kuala Lumpur."

"Old man, is there more gold? Be warned that you must not lie or

I will open your throat with the point of this kris."

"I knew of no gold, not even that in the box. Gold is heavy, and you can see how this boat waddles high, puffed up with air. I have no gold, Hock Sen."

"So, the old philosopher knows my name. How unfortunate for him."

Upon hearing the thieves find his jewelry, Tuck had felt anger, but he had not been afraid until the moment Hock Sen discovered Din knew his name. Tuck had not known Din for long, but he had come to revere him.

Din had a way with humor as well as the strange ability to sail the Straits without a compass. Tuck's dealing for the making of his wedding jewelry in Medan had lead to meeting Din. The goldsmith looked at Tuck's ring and the stones of blue fire and said, "Not enough. Bring me more gold or buy it from me." Tuck lacked the money for the gold, so he bartered, as he had done for the stones: on the wharf where his junk was moored, he traded his ship's compass and a fine galvanized anchor for a ring another smuggler claimed to be pure gold. Without the compass, Tuck could not find his way safely across the straits, but no matter. He engaged the services of an old man, Din, who would guide him in exchange for passage to Malacca. For an anchor, Tuck tied a rope around a rock the size of his head. It held the boat, but not so well when the wind blew.

The small stones with much blue fire had cost Tuck weeks of carrying a consignment of rice wine. The larger ones that shone like the moon in darkness and glittered in flakes of blue and red in the sunlight cost another trip across the straits, his junk loaded low in the water with hemp. The goldsmith accepted six rattan chairs for his work, chairs that represented the profit from another run across the waters between Malaya and Sumatra. "Still not enough gold," the goldsmith said when Tuck handed him the ring that cost a compass and an anchor. "I can stretch the gold with copper, if you do not mind lower-carat gold." Tuck agreed to the mixing of copper after being assured that the jewelry would still be valuable and rich with the color of gold.

When he set sail with Din, the old man asked why they sailed empty. "I must return to marry," Tuck said.

"But another five days, maybe a week, and you could go back with your junk loaded with something to make the trip worth taking. Life is long. Sometimes marriage seems even longer. A week is nothing to the tedious afternoons of listening to a wife."

Tuck explained he had just completed the work necessary to get the wealth he had to have for marriage, that he did not want to wait longer. He worked the sea not for money but for the ceremonial gold and gemstones so necessary in a proper marriage.

"The woman is expensive, then," Din said. "In Malacca, it is often thus. A man could work himself nearly to death for the gold required to bedeck the body of a Malaccan woman. It is not so in Siam. Forget the expensive woman, Tuck. Go to Siam. There they do not believe in dowry, and a man can marry for as little as one dollar and sixty cents. I have heard that the men of Khota Bharu often cross the border for such women."

Tuck looked at Din, unsure how to take this advice. Din returned his look with a solemn face, then lifted his brows and allowed the shadow of a smile. Tuck grinned.

"Of course, you are right," he said. "Finding a wife thus would be forever a lesson in frugality to my sons. When they asked why their mother was Siamese and not Chinese, I could say, 'Thrift, thrift. Were I a man to squander money, you would have an expensive Chinese mother, but your father is no fool to be cheated of his wealth with buying a wastrel and frivolous woman. Women of Siam are much cheaper to be had, and almost as pretty.' Thus could they be lessoned with proper values early in life."

"A fine lesson it would be, even to your daughters, teaching them not to demand so much gold lest they be outbid by the women of the north, come time for mating." Din had lifted his brows again, pleased with Tuck for his fine and understated humor. Tuck had enjoyed Din's fooleries, and liked the man. So the pirate's threat caused Tuck to tense with fear for him.

"But I have known your name for years, Mr. Tan Hock Sen," Din said, "so what does it matter? I will tell no one."

"True." Tuck heard a wet thump and some gurgling sounds, then saw Din pitch into the sea beside him. The body sank a meter or so, then floated to the surface, the water around it becoming dark. Tuck knew if there were more light, the water would carry a pink cloud around Din's head. "Set the fire there," Hock Sen said, "in the sheets of the old sail. Come. We return to Malacca."

"Din," Tuck whispered, watching the lifeless shape of the old man drift away from the junk. He forced back tears and felt a hot flash of anger surge through him, stirring a desire for vengeance. He forced back the anger, too, for the moment demanded all his craft, just to stay alive.

Tuck feared sharks being attracted to the blood, and he feared the fire sinking the junk. But right then he feared Hock Sen even more, so he stayed in the water while the pirates returned to their own boat.

As the other junk sailed into the night, Tuck pulled himself onto the deck. He removed his shirt and cast it upon the fire smoldering in the folded sail.

He found the sail damaged but usable. It was a simple matter to follow the pirate junk, keeping its cookfire in sight, and, later, the lamps Hock Sen and his men burned into the small hours of the night. Somewhere near morning, the thieves extinguished the lamps, and Tuck sailed on, blind, hoping he would not turn south and drift far into the Straits.

While he followed the men who killed Din, Tuck pondered his desire for avenging the death of the old man. It seemed so right to be angry for the way Hock Sen killed such a fine person and threw him to the crabs and sharks, like garbage. But Tuck knew his anger came also from losing the jewelry. "Do I want vengeance for Din or for myself?" he asked. The question gave him much discomfort.

And, he wondered, could I drive the blade of a kris into Hock Sen's neck? He tried to imagine it: the feel of flesh parting, the spurt of blood, and life quivering into the stillness of death there at the end of his knife.

No. He could not do it. Then he remembered Din floating in the sea and thought perhaps he could do it. But would such an act be right?

He thought of Hock Sen's children. Would they be better off without such a father? Could Tuck make that decision for them? He shrank from the thought of such responsibility. And what of Hock Sen's other children, those yet unborn? Tuck wondered. Would I not be murdering them, and their children on forever into times to come, and would not my act be murder multiplied among innocents?

When light came and Tuck found he sailed beside the coast, just kilometers north of Malacca, he had come to a decision. He could not feel right about killing Hock Sen, not in the cold light of day. He knew himself capable of the act, hot and angry from feeling the loss of Din and of the jewelry. But how to stay angry forever? He could not, and he knew the sense of right that came with anger would vanish with passing hours, leaving only bitterness and self reproach for an evil act.

But the desire for revenge still filled him, and he struggled to understand what to do with the feeling.

When Tuck reached Malacca, he sailed into the river and tied the junk to the dock belonging to Lim Kok Loon. Tuck longed to see Anita, but could not go to her. Months of work vanished when Hock Sen took the fire stones and gold, and Tuck could not tell her of more delay in marriage. He knew she would understand, and even in her disappointment she would offer him comfort. Such a woman. Months of hard and dangerous work were nothing to a life of marriage with her.

Tuck accepted his freedom to court and win Anita as his good luck. It troubled him, though, that such luck seemed based upon war, upon the loss of family wealth and pride, and upon the death of his father. Had the Japanese not disrupted life in Malacca, Tuck would never have sought the company of Anita, no matter how appealing he found her. He would have submitted to marrying the woman his parents chose, a Chinese woman, and a stranger.

Even in the ceremony of marriage, Tuck would not be able to see much of the face of the stranger who was in the process of becoming his mate for life, for her face would be obscured by a veil of beads hanging from the ceremonial wedding hat. Only when the time came for the couple to go into the bedroom would Tuck see her, illuminated by the candles on either side of the bed.

Better, Tuck told himself, far better to learn to love first, as he and Anita had done, then go through the ceremonies that would bind them together. But even as he told himself the new way was better, he felt guilt for abandoning the old ways.

When Tuck got home, he felt relief that his mother was out. He bathed and changed clothes, then found one of his mother's pins, which he threaded into the cuff of his pants. He took a fine, sharp *parang*, secured it under his belt, and went to the open market, where he bought a strait piece of rotan. He returned to his junk and spent some hours carving a walking stick from the rotan and fastening a handle on one end to lean upon. On a scrap of paper from a brown bag, Tuck wrote a message, drawing the Chinese characters with elaborate care.

When evening came, he limped, leaning upon the cane, through the narrow streets near the docks to look into tea houses and restaurants in search of Hock Sen.

Tuck found him in the Sin Yit Sing Restaurant, a noodle house where Hock Sen sat dipping chopsticks into a bowl and speaking with other men at his table. Finding a table near the door, Tuck sat and ordered jasmine cha. He studied the bottom of his cup, seeming to ignore Hock Sen and everyone else in the restaurant.

Five cups of cha later, Tuck watched Hock Sen leave. Tuck stood, stretched, and took the cane in hand to hobble out, seeming in no hurry to go anywhere. As soon as he turned the corner into the darkness, he stopped and watched the shadowy figure that was Hock Sen move in the direction of the wharves along the river. Tuck sprinted down another street, rounded a corner, and crouched in the shadows close to a small altar beside the wall of a building. An old woman bent over the altar, placing lighted joss sticks into a brass bowl. She stood, clasped her hands, bowed and mumbled a prayer.

The old woman had just wandered off toward the bridge when Hock Sen turned the corner, as Tuck knew he must in order to go to his junk. When he walked close, Tuck swung the cane hard and heard the sharp crack as it hit Hock's shin.

Hock grunted and fell forward, landing almost in front of the altar. Tuck leaped upon him, planted a knee on his back, took his hair in one hand and slammed his head against the cobblestones.

The body went limp. Tuck took it by its feet and dragged it away from the altar, into the shadows. Hock Sen breathed in shallow rasps, and Tuck felt relief that the man lived. He took his *parang* from his belt and snagged it into the pocket of Hock Sen's shirt, opening the pocket with a quick rip of cloth. But it held nothing. It would be so easy, Tuck thought, to open Hock Sen's throat as he had opened the pocket. He ran the *parang* up to the man's neck and thought of Din floating in the water. But I came not to kill, Tuck affirmed, holding the blade against Hock Sen's throat.

It was that moment when he saw the glint of gold and the sparkle from the stone, and Tuck realized with a sick feeling in his stomach that the pirate had put one of Anita's earrings in his own ear. Tuck's fist tightened on the handle of the knife, and he drew it across the neck, leaving a thin, shallow scratch that produced beads of blood.

He was amazed that his hand had not pushed the knife deep into the flesh. After taking the earring, Tuck slit open the pockets on Hock Sen's pants. The silk purse fell from one of them. Tuck opened it, removed a wad of paper, and thrust his finger inside, finding the other jewelry.

The wad of paper, he realized, was money, much money. More than Tuck made in months. He held it up to the light and thought of taking it. "But I am no thief," he whispered. He remembered the Chinese proverb that it was not stealing to take from a thief, and again the money tempted him.

But, he argued, if I take the stolen money, then I become guilty of stealing from those Hock Sen victimized. Yet if I leave the money, I allow him to enjoy the riches that are not his to enjoy. Decide, he commanded, for soon someone will come by, and I will be taken for a common thief.

He stuffed the money under Hock Sen's belt. Taking his mother's pin from his cuff, he attached the paper with his message to the front of the pirate's shirt.

"Tuck went home," Weng said, "where he spent much time washing the earring, for it seemed to Tuck that Hock Sen had debased and dishonored it by thrusting it upon his ear." Weng fell silent. Allen waited until it became clear the old man considered his story finished.

"The message," Allen asked, "pinned to the shirt—what did it say?"

Weng shook his head. "Bad. A terrible message. Perhaps Tuck would have done less damage by leaning hard on the knife when he scratched Hock Sen's throat, for Tuck had written, 'Know that Din, the Philosopher of Labuhanbilik, has made his first attack upon your body. Other attacks will come, subtle and more damaging, upon your evil pirate's spirit.' Tuck thought himself clever for finding a way to get vengeance for Din, but he came to regret writing those words. Mr. Tan Hock Sen lived a miserable life after that night, to be sure. He did give up going to sea and preying upon the defenseless ones in the Straits of Malacca. That was good, his reformation from being a pirate. But he gave his family misery, beating his wife and children, speaking kindness to no one. It seemed as if he knew himself cursed, so he determined to make everyone around him suffer for it. He drove his wife into an early grave, and his sons ran away, becoming rogues and thieves. His daughters went to Kuala Lumpur where, many said, they sold themselves each night. It was not good, what Tuck did, and his vengeance tasted bitter in his mouth."

"He married Anita?"

Weng's face brightened. "Yes. In a ceremony with proper jewelry. She lived long and happy in his home and died without regrets for having married outside of the Portuguese settlement."

"And this," Allen held up the ring with three opals full of fire, "was her wedding ring. A fine story, Mr. Chee Tuck Weng, and I thank you for telling it."

Yim Choy jerked his head up. "You?" he demanded, "You were the young man in the story? You are Tuck?"

Tuck and Allen held eye contact, ignoring Yim Choy. "The woman I am married to," Allen said, "is named Ana, and those in the Portugese colony would call her Anita. I would be honored to present her with this jewelry as a gift for our wedding anniversary."

"Your wife? Anita? You know, of course, the meaning of the word. Graceful. Anita Chee, she chose to call herself. Such a wonderful and graceful woman. This anniversary gift, is it a custom among Americans?"

"Yes."

"A ceremony, then, this giving of jewelry for celebrating the continuing of marriage. Ah, a fine tradition. I would be pleased, Mr. Allen Harrison, if you would take my Anita's jewelry as a gift for your Anita. A gift from me and from the spirit of my wife."

"No," Allen said, moved by the offer. "That would not feel right to me. I must pay, though there is no way I could pay the high price you paid. Please do not be offended."

Chee Tuck Weng nodded. "We do what we must with traditions."

"Now," Allen said, "it is time for me to speak with Yim Choy in the ceremony of negotiation for the price of this fine jewelry."

Book Club Discussion Questions

1. Why did Reed cry at the Malaysian burial in "A Man He Had Never Known?"

2. When the author sent the story "Shadow Man" to a Malaysian literary magazine, the editor said he would not dare publish the story because some leaders of the Malaysian government could be displeased and might punish the staff of the journal for publishing the story.

     What in the story might governmental officials have found offensive?

3. What was the meaning of *choice* as Cheong Lee Chin used the term at the end of "An Odor of Durian?"

4. What are the possible causes of Trish losing her memory in "Caught by Memory?"

5. The *Merriam-Webster Dictionary* defines *culture shock* as "a sense of confusion and uncertainty sometimes with feelings of anxiety that may affect people exposed to an alien culture or environment without adequate preparation."

     Of all the characters in the 11 stories, which suffers most from culture shock?

6. Which of the stories uses darkness as a symbol for or a suggestion about death?

7. Characters in each of the stories undergo change. Name two characters taken from two different stories who change the most and explain your choices.

8. Tich Nhat Hanh wrote: "Mindfulness is the energy that helps us recognize the conditions of happiness that are already present in our lives. You don't have to wait ten years to experience this happiness. It is present in every moment of your daily life. There are those of us who are alive but don't know it."

     One of the concepts examined in several of the stories is mindfulness. Name 3 characters (and explain your choices) who embrace mindfulness or struggle to do so.